The Christmas Bell: A Horror Novel

L.A. Detwiler

Published by L.A. Detwiler, 2020.

This is a work of fiction. Similarities to real people, places, or events are entirely coincidental.

THE CHRISTMAS BELL: A HORROR NOVEL

First edition. November 10, 2020.

ISBN: 978-1393816874

Written by L.A. Detwiler.

To all of my readers. Thank you for embracing the darkness with me.

Prologue

The tree glowed with the traditional lights, a symbolic beacon of brightness amidst the horror that had become her life. She stared at them, wishing she could disappear into the vast number of bulbs on the strand. Wishing she could feel them burn her from the inside out. She wondered if her guilt would crumble with the ashes of her flesh, or if it would, in fact, remain long after the semblance of who she was incinerated.

In the distance, she could hear the Christmas carolers belting out the words to "Silent Night," but they grated on her nerves. This was not a holy night—it never would be again. This was a night tinged by sorrow, regret, and guilt.

Sorrow for the death of her twin that she painted on her face.

Regret for the part she played.

And guilt—not for the thing she had done, but for the fact that within her core, buried underneath the superficial sorrow and grief and sadness, something else remained.

Joy. Season's joy, yearlong joy at the fact that she was finally gone. Her greatest tormentor, her greatest fear was gone from this world. She was finally dead.

1

"Dear, they found this in her things. I didn't want to give it you, but Father said we should. It was her final wish, after all."

She turned to look at her mother, or the being who somewhat resembled her mother. After the past few day's events, she knew that her mother would never exist the same way again either. Sure, she would paint on that faux smile outlined with red lips as she baked pies and went to the women's choir practice and talked at the supermarket to her friends about upcoming charities. But behind every story, every lie, there would always be the ugly truth that everyone recognized but couldn't admit. They had failed as a family. They had failed as parents. And Anne had failed as a sister.

Her eyes fell now from the gray, pallid skin of her mother's tear-stained face to her trembling hands. They looked so wrinkled, so unappealing, as they stretched toward her with the item. It was wrapped in a crumpled piece of notebook paper, the kind that is too thin to be of any substance or natural looking. It was crudely taped around a spherical object, pieces of the translucent tape sporadically placed, as if the wrapper had been in a hurry. The gift lacked finesse and certainly wasn't one Mother would ever put under the perfectly decorated tree on a normal year. But this was no normal year.

Anne stared at her name hurriedly written in a frenetic scrawl on the front of the tiny package. Sobs threatened to rack her body. She was glad Rachel was gone in so many ways—but there was still something haunting about touching an item that belonged to a girl who didn't know what fate awaited her.

Or did she? That was something she would push aside for now. She took the package from her mother, choosing to wander to her room to open the final gift. She was surprised her mother granted her this courtesy. Perhaps her mother had already decided, however, to wash her hands of this delicate, vile matter. Her mother in her stark white apron and adeptly curled hair—it wouldn't do to dirty her face with tinges of the truth. It wouldn't do at all. She would leave that to Anne, just as she had done back in July.

In her room, perched on her bed, Anne tediously peeled back the layers. Had Rachel really thought this far ahead? She had never been close to her, especially after what happened in July. Why would she decide to leave her a gift now? Was it a final parting, a final remedy for a life that was lived in the recesses of wickedness?

As her fingers pulled back the paper, she knew there was no gift that could assuage her cruelty, could save her soul from the torments she must be facing. Lives are filled with mistakes—but Rachel's had been filled with fiendish feats performed with remarkable malevolence too filthy to be wiped clean.

When the paper was removed, she studied the metal object in her hands. A bell sat in her hands, a rusty red color. She placed a hand over her mouth, shaking. The bell was familiar. She'd seen it once before but had thought nothing of it. She'd thought it nothing more than her overactive imagination mixing trauma and Christmas together.

But here it was, real in all ways. It was covered in scratches as if someone's fingernails had dug away until the rusty metal underneath peeked through. She looked closer, leaning in to see a hooded girl carved on the front of the bell, remarkable detail embossed in the surface. She looped a finger through the twine, flipping the ornament between her fingers to examine it closer. As the bell twirled between her fingers, rotating, she noticed that the back didn't match the front. On the back side of the ornament, a message was carved.

And when she read the words carved in the festive adornment, a foreboding gloom drowned her until she was gasping for air. A dread like she'd never felt swept through her veins, clawing at her skin until she could scarcely remember who she was. She choked on sobs, crumpling to the ground. A ringing in her brain drowned out all her awareness.

As she looked once more at the words, she knew she wasn't imagining it. For where words such as Noel or Happy Holidays or Good Tidings should have been, a dire warning of the most menacing kind was clawed into the surface of the metal. She knew who it was from. She knew what it meant. She just didn't know what the consequences would be.

But when her eyes finally unlocked from the carved words, she saw it. Across the bedroom, near the corner. And as her heart beat wildly, words frozen in her throat, she knew that she wasn't actually safe at all . . . and that the sinister occurrences were probably only beginning.

Christmas and all its joys had morphed into a Darker Christmas Spirit—one that there was no celebrating and certainly no escaping from.

At the realization, she tossed the ornament across the room, only to notice that where the twine had been, a bloody cut was now seeping on her finger. She watched the red droplets fall, knowing that the White Christmas the carolers sang about outside their home had turned to red.

Horrifying, fiendish red.

Chapter One
Candace

Her car creaking to a dusty stop in front of the familiar Cape Cod on the hill that she'd always called home but no longer could, Candace Mills realized that the adage was true—you could never really go home again after being gone so long, especially when everything was different. True, the neighboring houses on Maple Street were still the same, in so many ways. The familiar lights still graced the houses, the trees. The same streetlights, the same shutters, the same lawns sat in disarray. It was all so normal, but not in a comforting way—in a dull, sleepy way.

As she encroached on the lane leading to her driveway, the house came into sight. Her childhood home still had the same dilapidated green door that she used to think looked like vomit, and the shutter on the bottom right corner was still cracked in half. She looked at the house perched back a winding dirt lane, offset from the other cookie cutter houses on the street. It was guarded by trees and distance, a distance Candace had felt growing up when all the kids had called her house the creepy one. Looking at it objectively now that time and distance had passed, Candace could agree. There was something melancholic, different about the house that sat back far enough to be aloof but close enough to be considered an unwanted nuisance.

So many things about 1119 Maple Street were still the same—but why, then, did she feel like Christmas was going to be anything but the same? Why did she feel as she forced her squeaky, creaking bones out of her car after the six-hour drive from the city, that a foreboding cloud of change lurked right above them all?

She wiped her weary eyes as she gathered her few bags from the backseat and the sack of presents for her mother and grandmother. She was tired, road weary after the long trek alone. Always alone now. And maybe that right there was it. Maybe after Landon had left, she'd really fallen into the deep depression her mother accused her of over the phone on their weekly Sunday calls. Maybe everything that was the same just felt different now that her heart had been cracked in two, scorned by her first real love in the adult world. Or maybe she was just different altogether, leaving behind sleepy town life for the bustle of New York City. Oakwood didn't feel like home anymore because it many ways, it wasn't. She'd changed. She'd grown up. She'd moved on. She felt guilty as she walked through the door, the smell of cookies wafting to the entrance as her mother turned and smiled.

"Candace, sweetie, it's good to finally see you."

Candace reminded herself not to roll her eyes at her mother's pointed choice of words. It had been, after all, over a year and a half since she'd made it home. Life in the city as a struggling college grad wasn't easy, and working your way up the ladder in any company required devotion devoid of familial responsibilities. She brushed the thought aside as her mother wrapped her in a hug, the familiar floral scent from her childhood assaulting her nose. Some things didn't change after all.

"Candace?" the rickety voice beckoned from the kitchen. Her mother smiled, leaning in to whisper.

"She's been asking about you all afternoon. She's been excited to see you."

Candace felt guilt again assault her. It had been too long since she'd seen Grandma Anne. Way too long. She reminded herself that this was what convinced her to come home for the holidays, to tell Johnson & Company Design Elements that she was using her week of vacation to go home. After all, Grandma Anne wasn't doing well. Her failing mind and health required her to move here, with her daughter, after she couldn't keep up with her home anymore. Mom refused to let Grandma Anne move to a nursing home—she'd heard the horror stories, after all. So she'd instead singlehandedly moved Grandma Anne and her belongings from her tiny house an hour away in with her. Candace, of course, had been working. She pressed the guilt down once more.

This Christmas might be her last, a voice had plagued her as she'd sat at her computer two weeks ago in the office, working on a plan for a major client. She needed to get home. Last Christmas Landon had whisked her away to the Rockies for a romantic week in a snowy chamber. So it was due time she came home, no matter how depressing the house could be, no matter how frustrating her mother was.

"Come on, let's get you settled in with some coffee. My, you're looking thin. Are you eating over in New York?"

Candance grimaced but reminded herself to stay in the holiday spirit. She followed her mother into the tiny yet familiar kitchen, Grandma Anne perched on a chair. Candace softened at the sight of the elderly woman who peered at her behind her glasses. Memories of cookie baking and trips to the movies and the mall in her younger years pressed on her mind and heart, softening her Grinch-like spirit just a bit.

"Grandma," she murmured, her voice taking on a childlike quality once more. She leaned in to hug the sweet woman, noticing the fragility in her frame she didn't quite remember and tremors of the hand that weren't always there.

"Candace, dear. It's so good you're home for Christmas. Do you know I live here now?"

"Yes, Grandma. How are you liking it?" Candace leaned out of the hug and took a seat across from her.

Grandma Anne made a noise between a sputter and a cough. "Your mother insists I eat healthy foods for my heart. And she didn't let me bring all my stuff. I miss my trinkets, you know."

"Mom, you know we couldn't bring everything. The attic is already bursting."

"At least you let me bring Muffin," Grandma Anne retorted, referring to the diabetic black cat that she'd had since Candace was a teenager. At that, the goliath cat mewled at Candace's feet, transferring black hairs onto her gray leggings. She reached down to pet him as Grandma Anne continued on.

"So how is New York?" the elderly woman asked, and Candace filled her in on her career, on her successes, and gracefully skipped over all the struggles. She didn't need her mother having more ammunition as to why a twenty-six-year-old didn't need to live in a "dangerous" city like New York alone. That was a battle that had been waged too many times.

After small talk, the three women retired to bed, Candace being led my Marian Mills to the spare bedroom—her childhood room now overtaken by Grandma Anne and her myriad clothes, knick-knacks, and religious relics she refused to part with.

"How's she doing, really?" Candace asked her exhaustion-filled mother, worried that she was missing more than just daily banter by not being there.

"She has her good days and bad. The move was hard on her," Marian replied, offering a weak smile.

"And on you, too, I'm sure. I wish you would have let me send that moving company to help," Candace said. She hadn't told her mother that the offer would have required a hefty credit card bill she wouldn't have been able to pay.

"You know I like doing things myself."

"Still, it must've been a lot of work."

"It was," her mother admitted, sighing. Candace could see the wear of the years and of worry on her mother's once-smooth, supple face. "There are still a lot of boxes in the attic to go through."

"Maybe I can help with that," she offered.

"That would be great. I love you, sweetie."

"I love you, too, Mom."

She hugged her mother, kissing her on the cheek, holding on just a little longer than normal. So much had changed, but some things hadn't.

As she tucked herself into an unfamiliar bed in a familiar house, Candace told herself that this Christmas would be merry, bright, and blessed. But with her eyes closing and thoughts of the holidays spilling into her dreamlike state, she thought for a moment she heard something up above. A rustling, a movement, something.

She turned over, ignoring her overactive imagination. She told herself it was just being back in this house. The old memories were coming back. She needed to let it go. After all, he'd been gone for so many years. There was nothing to fear anymore.

Chapter Two
Candace

Sweat forming on her brow despite the bitter temperatures, Candace shoved another box aside in the cramped, dusty attic. The single bare bulb in the center of the room cast an overbearing glow on the items beneath it, highlighting every dirty crevice and forgotten box stacked in the claustrophobic area. As a girl, Candace had only braved creeping through the door in her mother's bedroom into the dirty space once—she'd stashed her yearbook with Johnny Kincaid's love note deep in the bowels of the unforgiving attic, hoping no one would ever see it but that it would still be safe. Back then, she'd been certain the boy would ask her to marry him and that they'd have the quintessential white-picket fence and 2.5 kids. All by twenty-five. What a fool she'd been.

Her arms ached as she slid over yet another box of Grandma Anne's porcelain doll collection. In her house, Grandad had built a beautiful display case to spotlight the frozen creatures and their hauntingly sweet smiles. Now, Candace's mother had apparently relinquished the miniature children to the recesses of the attic, soon to be forgotten as they soaked in the dusty, repulsive musk that Candace knew was already leaking into her hair.

Candace stood up too far, cracking her head on the low-hanging beam as she traversed the stacks to find the box she was looking for. Instantly, she whipped a hand through her hair, hoping to fling off any bat that certainly must be seeking refuge in the attic—or perhaps her paranoias from her childhood were just creeping in since she was home, surrounded by relics and usurped by unrelenting nostalgia. Convincing herself that no vermin had taken up a sanctuary in her nest of wavy hair, Candace pushed forward, fighting the urge to bolt from the attic and say forget it. Grandma Anne needed this. Her mother needed this. And it was the least she could do, all things considered. True, there were only three days until Christmas, so it seemed sort of pointless to go through all the hassle of assembling the tree. But if it could make Grandma Anne smile and even her mother, it would be worth the trouble.

With her mother and grandmother off to the store for some last-minute baking supplies, Candace had convinced herself to wrestle down the artificial tree, to bring some holiday spirit to the otherwise stark, plain home she'd once lived in. Sure, things weren't picture-perfect, with Grandma leaving her home and Landon—she stopped herself. She'd promised herself she wouldn't spend the whole week at home pining for something that couldn't be. She was a strong twenty-six-year-old. She had years and years to get that part of her life down—didn't she?

She blew a piece of hair out of her face, knowing she'd need a shower immediately after this to crush the fears that spiders had infested her clothes. Her fingers clawed through worn and weathered boxes, opening and closing them, revisiting happy and depressing moments from the past. Certainly Grandma Anne's Christmas decorations weren't left behind, were they?

She started to worry that her plan, like everything else in her life, would soon disintegrate like the plethora of dust coating every inch of the dank room. But then, just as she was ready to give up, she peeked into a box that held the ornaments she desperately sought. She smiled, picturing the red and green angel, the glitter-specked snowflakes, alight on Grandma's majestic tree. It was one of the happy memories of her childhood, one of the things not tainted by him. She folded the top of the box, turning to head back to the tiny door when she saw it and paused.

A miniscule box, unassuming, shoved in the back corner behind boxes and boxes of Grandma Anne's things. It was a dark brown box similar to the others but somehow more weathered and dingier. Nevertheless, it still maintained its perfect shape. It was duct taped numerous times and looked like it hadn't been opened in years, if not decades.

Candace set down the box in her arms, inexplicably drawn to the tiny box chucked in the back of the attic. Surrounded by so many of Grandma Anne's things, it was odd to be obsessed with this one, but she couldn't stop herself. Her feet trudged toward it, catching on a board. Candace hit her head on the beam, shouting strings of profanities that would make her mother and grandmother reprimand her, even at this age.

That was what she got for being too nosy, she thought to herself. Still, the box was within reach. She stretched, gripping the box with her weary fingers. As she lifted it and pulled it closer to see if an explanation was etched on top, she shrieked, dropping it on her foot. A spider, gnarly and frenetic, scurried across the box, across her hand, causing her to fling her limbs wildly. Her heart raced as she backed up, still whipping her hand as if the creature had latched on. When the real or imaginary prickling of its legs climbing up her arm stopped, she stooped down to reclaim the box.

"Hope it wasn't breakable," she murmured to the room, her heart still beating wildly. But as she held it, leaning in to look more closely at it, her stomach dropped again. Her heart raced, as if the spider was back. She was being ridiculous, she knew. Call it a lack of caffeine or just paranoia from being in the darkened, dirty recesses of the room she always feared. Whatever it was, she knew she needed to get out of there and back into the light of day.

She put the small box on top of the other one, carrying it downstairs to start getting things ready for when Grandma and Mom returned. Tonight, she'd set aside all the doubts and past hurts and frustrations and fears. She'd celebrate like the best of them, and help Grandma Anne remember her past traditions, too. She'd help deck out the tree with Grandma Anne's favorite ornaments, an ode to the past meeting the present, to generational traditions being forged together as one.

After emerging from the darkened attic, she carried the treasures downstairs. She set the boxes down in the living room by the artificial tree she'd already managed to rig together. She perused the small box once more, finding it a spot on the floor near the back of the tree.

Odd. She hadn't noticed the writing upstairs, the looping letters in dark black that hadn't faded one bit on the top flap of the box.

One too many.

That was all it said. What could that mean? Candace shook her head. Grandma clearly wasn't thinking as straight as Mom would like to believe. Candace was almost terrified to open the box. Who knew what would be inside? For all she knew, it could be a dead bird or an old pudding cup as crazy as Grandma Anne had been sometimes, according to her mother's phone calls. She turned the box over in her hands, an eerie sensation flooding her limbs once more. She shook it. It sounded heavy, jingly. Peculiar.

She started picking at the corner of duct tape, ready to reveal the contents of the box that was probably nothing. It was taking up way too much of her time and imagination. As she peeled the strip back, ready to open the box, she jumped.

The doorbell. She sighed, setting the box down, wondering who could possibly be coming for a visit.

The mystery would have to wait . . . because someone was insistent on getting in. And for a second, Candace shuddered as she always did when someone unidentified was at the door. Old habits die hard, after all.

Chapter Three
Candace

"Surprise!" the familiar voice announced, and Candace sighed in relief at the sight of Rosalie and Eva, all bundled up in protection against the blowing snow.

"Hey," she replied warmly, leaning in to wrap both of her high school friends in a hug.

"I brought the wine since I'm off duty," Eva announced as the two strutted through the door, leading themselves to the familiar kitchen where they'd spent plenty of time in their younger years.

"It's so good to see you two," Candace said as she led them to the table, grabbing wine glasses from the cupboard and reminding herself it would be okay. It was just a glass, after all. Not like before. Never like before. Rosalie unwrapped her scarf, draping it over the wooden chair that she'd always claimed as hers when she was over.

"Your mom saw me at the grocery store yesterday. She told me you were coming in today," Rosalie said as she sat in the chair. That sounded like Candace's mother—always insistent, always nosy. But this time, Candace didn't mind.

"Are you back in town?" Candace asked, remembering that Rosalie had left for Ohio a few years ago.

"Yep. Taking over the accounting practice. I just got a house nearby. Your mother's friend, Kim, actually sold it to me."

Candace grinned. Her mother always knew everyone's business.

"And your mother saw my mother at church, of course," Eva said. She'd never left Oakwood after high school, settling straight into her EMT job. Her fiancé, Pat, had family nearby, too, and insisted they stay. Eva was always dreaming of leaving, of seeing distant shores. Candace knew she never would. She was the dreamer who never found her wings. Of course, finding your wings didn't guarantee that you'd find that distant shore or blue skies or anything even close.

"It's good to be here, together, isn't it?" Rosalie said, and they all nodded as Eva poured the wine. It was odd, in some ways. They hadn't really kept close touch other than the occasional message on social media or random text. They'd seen each other a few times over the years, but life, as it had a way of doing, had stretched them in different directions, pulled them toward different people. Candace could feel a familiarity tinged by the coldness that distance and time often bring.

Candace was just preparing to ask Rosalie about her new house when the door opened again, cold air pelting into them.

"Oh, good! I had an intuition you two would be here. Didn't I, Mother?" Marian said to Grandma Anne, who was bundled up like a kindergartner out in the first snow of the year.

"What?" Grandma Anne cawed, her arms constricted by several grocery bags as Marian carried in three pizzas.

"I got extra just because I knew. Candace, help Grandma with those bags while I get everything ready." Marian's hostess face emerged as she hurriedly unbundled and set to work clearing spaces and offering sodas and idle chit chat.

Candace assisted Grandma Anne as her mother fell back in gracefully to the familiar hosting dance she clearly missed. She grabbed the nice plates, a wedding gift from Grandma Anne that were too expensive for her to toss when things went sour. She asked warm questions in her sing-song voice that used to make Candace roll her eyes. Rosalie and Eva were gracious as ever, answering questions about boyfriends and fiancés and even Rosalie's new shade of red hair. Despite the annoying quality, it felt good to be in a house with the familiar comforts from the past. If she was honest, going home to that apartment in Brooklyn wasn't comforting. She pictured the cold walls now devoid of the photographs of their memories. She imagined the pair of shoes he'd left in the corner that she just couldn't bring herself to throw away.

Weak woman, she internally scolded herself. She'd been raised by her mother to be strong, independent. But she had failed. She was fragile, pining for a man who wasn't worth pining for any longer.

Dinner passed without incident, and Candace committed half-heartedly to the conversation, to the jokes, to Grandma Anne's mildly confusing questions. When it was over and Eva and Rosalie appeared restless to escape to their own familiars, Marian spoke up on her return from a bathroom trip.

"What's all of that in the living room, Candace?" she asked, lacking the hint of frustration she usually did when things weren't going according to her plan.

"Oh. Well, it seems senseless now. But I thought it would be nice to put up a tree, make it a bit festive around here. And I found some of Grandma Anne's decorations, you know, so she could feel at home."

"Oh, my ornaments! My decorations. Wonderful. Just wonderful. So many years of that beautiful tree. Yes, let's. Can we, sweetheart?" Grandma Anne asked excitedly, clapping her hands. It was good to see a smile on her face, one Candace had incited.

"Of course. Rosalie, Eva, why don't you stay for a little longer? I'll make some hot cocoa. It'll be like old times."

"You don't have to," Candace retorted, not wanting them to feel pressure. They weren't the same as they had been. Time had grown between them. She didn't want them feeling obliged to stay.

"It's fine. I wouldn't mind. Pat's Menorah is nice and all, but it's no Christmas tree. And between my long shifts, I haven't had the energy to decorate," Eva replied. Candace wasn't sure if it was the truth or if it was the second glass of wine talking.

"I suppose I could stay for a little bit," Rosalie said, twirling her hair. It was clear staying was the last thing on her mind. She was dressed to kill and probably had some fabulous invitation or elite bar to visit, looking for Mr. Right. But she had always been apologetic, fearful of conflict.

With that, the crew of women moved into the living room, where Marian began frantically unpacking boxes, barking orders, and managing to turn even tree decorating into an assembly line with pointed instructions and rules. Still, Grandma Anne smiled as ornament after ornament stirred a memory, a story, a feeling. It was as if the décor told the tale of Grandma Anne's life, of the generations of smiles and hardships. It was a living tribute to the woman's history, one Candace was fascinated to hear more about.

When all the ornaments were on the tree, Candace glanced to the corner and remembered the box with the odd phrase. She'd forgotten to peek inside with the commotion of the guests stopping her in the middle of it. Wine dulling her senses, she pushed past the guests to the corner.

"There's one more box that was up there. I'm not sure what it is," Candace mentioned as she reached for the box. She turned to face the group, the glow of the Christmas tree adding a softness to the scene, as if they were on some holiday commercial.

But as she slowly parted the crease of the box, finishing the job she'd stopped earlier, an inexplicable dread crawled into her skin, her bones, her stomach. Her fingers clumsily dug into the box, rejecting her body's repulsion. It was ridiculous, she knew. It was only a box.

Her fingers brushed against a scratchy metal. Rosalie, Marian, Eva, and Anne stared on as she lifted a red bell from the box, rusty and scratched. As she lifted it high for all to see, though, her head began to spin, the Christmas lights whirling in a concoction reflective of a twisted, nauseating carnival ride that you can't wait to get off. The lights were too bright, pounding, grating her skull. Her hair stood on end on her arms, and her stomach lurched violently as if the wine and pizza were about to spew.

She thought something must be happening, an earthquake of some sort or a medical emergency. *Everyone else must feel it, too,* she thought, as the room remained unsteady, as her fingers ached at the touch of the twine on the bell. As the flashes of images began. Blurry pictures of red, of screams, of long black hair down a skinny, bony back. Grimy, tiled rooms and scissors in her face. It was all marred by a haze of red, as if her eyes were bloody. She shook her head, feeling like vomiting but unable to even respond in that way. Her hands trembled crazily, her whole body quaking against her will.

"Candace?" a voice beckoned as reality interrupted the flashes in her head. Her mother reached out, grabbing the ornament and passing it over to Eva. Her mother, who had clutched onto Candace's arm at the sight of trouble, let go to touch her own head, a grimace momentarily painted on her face. She shook her head as if shaking off a leaf that had fallen in her hair, her face scrunched up but the look quickly passing. The room steadied for Candace, her head still aching.

"Candace, are you okay? What's wrong? You look pale. Sit down, what's wrong?" Her mother's hands wrapped around her arms. She was thankful for the steadying she got from her mother, but she was confused. Dazed. Everything was back to normal. What happened? She'd had too much wine. That was it. It had been so long since she'd had a glass, since the last time when things went terribly, terribly wrong. She was probably just being paranoid, thinking about what had happened last time.

"I'm fine, I'm fine. Just a dizzy spell," Candace insisted. This was a mistake because instantly, her mother started talking about doctors and eating enough and all sorts of things. But there wasn't time for Candace to answer.

"Shit, shit, shit," Eva mumbled, her hand now trembling as she wobbled on her feet. Instinctually, Rosalie reached out for the ornament, and Eva steadied, her face pale and her eyes wide as if she'd seen a ghost.

Candace studied her, wondering if she'd seen it, wondering if the red and the grimy tile had manifested in her mind too. It was crazy, fucking crazy. She was really losing it, just like Landon had accused. She *was* batshit mad.

Just as she was ready to relinquish the fact that she was ever going to be okay again, stable, Rosalie also started to tremble, the red bell shaking in her hand. Being closest to the tree, she turned and flung it on a branch. The red bell swayed on the branch gently until finally, it settled on its new home.

The five women stared at the bell marked by a strange image of a hooded girl, staring at it forlornly as if they'd all just walked through a fire together yet also alone. They studied the ornament, the lights around it seeming to dull. Nothing glittered quite the same, as if a dark fog had descended on the once immaculate, cheery tree. Candace met everyone's eyes. It was if they all wanted to speak, to admit what they'd seen but couldn't say the words for fear of being crazy.

"I think it's time to put away the wine," Marian declared, of course being the first one to speak up.

"Yes, I think it's time I go," Rosalee murmured, and Eva was quick to agree. The women convinced themselves that they had each singlehandedly experienced some sort of mental glitch, some sort of brain misfiring, some sort of inebriated hallucination.

They would have all went to bed brushing aside their fears and the odd visions that night. They would have attributed it to the potent alcohol or the exhaustion from travelling and baking and shopping or anything but the ornament.

Except Grandma Anne wasn't ready to let it go so quickly.

She had been the only one who hadn't touched the ornament, but by the way she stared at it from her chair, Candace thought that she, too, must have once felt it in her hands. Her eyes were locked on the single bell, an unwavering, unblinking gaze that dripped with melancholy. She rocked in the wooden chair that wasn't meant for rocking, a pace too fast for an aging woman and a rigid, squeaking chair. She stared, her lips slowly moving as if in a silent prayer. It was only when Candace moved closer that she could hear the faint words whispered over and over again.

"Wretched girl. Wretched girl. Wretched girl."

"Come along, Mother. I think you're worn out," Marian sang way too cheerily, grabbing the elderly woman's arm. But as Marian walked Anne back the hall, the old woman spun her head, as if she was afraid to turn her back on the ornament.

Eva and Rosalie looked at Candace.

"Maybe you should put the ornament away," Eva whispered. Candace had already considered it. But there was one major problem.

She wasn't quite ready to reach out and touch the enigmatic bell again for fear it might confirm the truth—there was something severely wrong with the ornament, something dark about it.

Chapter Four
Anne

Wretched girl. Wicked girl. Cursed girl.
The words flipped in the crevices of her brain, threatening to break free. They danced through her head, trying to spew from her tongue of their own volition. They were committed to a memory that was failing but still stayed true in some form—even if she didn't know what it meant. Wretched girl. But who? Somewhere deep within, a name, a face, a memory tried to break free. She grabbed her head, willing it forward. If she could just loosen the phrase, remember what it meant. Maybe it would all be okay.

The tree was covered with glittering mementos of the happy times, perched on the branches like magnificent signs of the season. But somehow, around the one that Candace had unearthed from the attic, the branches seemed darker. They seemed to drown under the pressure of that paradoxically light and heavy ornament, bending to its will.

Staring at the ornament spotlighted in the middle of the other traditional decor, her hands furled into fists and trembled. Nausea overpowered her, and a familiar feeling unfamiliarly crept into her veins. It had been so long—how long? She couldn't tell. Perhaps her brain had tucked away the images, the sensations, the dread long ago when the scratched, weathered ornament had been locked away to be forgotten. She ached to reach out and touch the ornament, but she couldn't bring herself too close. A dark aura floated from the tree, pushing her away like a forcefield. Like the child drawn to the outlet with the fork in her hand, she was pulled to it, afraid to see what doom would be unleashed if she did—but also dying to have an end to it just the same. That was what it was. Deep within her chest, despite her always muddled mind, there was a protection surging within. She needed to protect them. She needed to keep them safe. They were all that mattered, especially now.

How could she, though? And what could she do to stop it all? She didn't know, her head hurting with too many swirling memories and fragments that just didn't seem to piece together.

Staring at the tree, nonetheless, the ornaments taking on a murky haze, something ripped loose. Her mind might be failing, but the sense of dread in her gut was still strong. Perusing the tree as her chest heaved, Anne knew that the ornament—it was one too many. And maybe they all were, too. She never wanted two, after all. No one ever wanted two.

Chapter Five
Anne
1948

*S*ome said she had been deprived of oxygen since Anne was born first and she had been left in the womb, an unwanted surprise lurking in the cavern of her mother's body. Others said it had something to do with being dropped by the doctor when she made her grand entrance to a world not ready for a girl like her. Still others said that she was just born bad, like an apple rotten from the center as soon as it falls from the tree. But Anne knew the truth. She'd heard the story whispered in the darkness by the candlelight as her mother chanted the words, asking why it hadn't worked. Asking God if he had other plans. Asking when it would be time to get rid of the cursed child.

One too many. Rachel had always been one too many.

Ten-year-old Anne played with her doll in the corner of their shared room, snowflakes falling outside of the window of their tiny house. She blocked out the screams in the kitchen, the slapping, Rachel's threats echoing above it all. She no longer fretted over her sister's maniacal actions or Mama's wild reactions. It was sad, but *true. In ten years, Anne had just grown numb to her twin sister's volatile behaviors. So she kept playing, imagining a life where the room was all hers, where the toys were all hers, and where her mother was happy with the single child she wanted.*

One too many. Rachel would always be one too many.

Something crashed in the kitchen, and Rachel came flying back into the room. Her chest heaved, her body shaking with anger.

"Are you kidding me? You're just going to sit there while she does this to me? Can't you see how horrible she is, Anne? Can't you see?"

Anne put down the doll, taking a deep breath. She reminded herself that Rachel was just like this, and when she got like this, there was no talking her down. She thought about asking Rachel what she'd done this time to get Mother so mad. Last week, there had been the neighbor's cat that Rachel claimed walked in front of her too quickly. They all suspected a darker truth. There had also been the incident with Melissa last week and the scissors to her hair. Rachel swore it wasn't her.

That was the problem, though. It was never her fault. Rachel lacked culpability. That was what Mother and Dad always said. Rachel claimed they just never wanted to take her side and that they hated her. She said she was the victim.

But every monster thinks they're the victim, *Anne thought as Rachel babbled threats, her voice an octave too high like it always was when she got like this.*

Anne turned now, looking at her black-haired sister. Too pale. Too gangly. Too wild. No one ever even knew they were twins. Anne prided herself on staying polished, neat, ready to face the day with a smile. She knew even at ten that she needed to protect her reputation and her standing if she wanted to have a suitable husband someday. Rachel didn't worry about these things, looking like a mangey, untamed creature. They were as opposite as opposite could be.

And, even though she'd never announce it, she also felt like they were of a different caliber. Anne was better than Rachel, just like Mother always said. How couldn't she be? Anne didn't hurt animals or lie or steal or any of the other psychotic things Rachel did. Anne was the good child. She prided herself on that reputation.

Mama was right. Rachel was one too many. Mama had never wanted twins. One child. One perfect child to pamper. Rachel had been an extra, a mistake, an unwanted surprise. Mama made that clear time and time again. And did Rachel really think that her behavior was proving her wrong?

Anne turned to her shaking sister, and calmly, politely, offered the only assurance she could. "You better calm down. You don't want them sending you back again, do you?"

She'd meant it to be a subtle reassurance, a warning. But it did something to Rachel. It lit something in her, an ugly fire that smoldered and then raged.

"You wretch. I'm not going back there. I'm not. You love this, don't you? You love being the favorite. It won't last forever, Anne. Even the underdog rises up sometimes. Remember that when you're sleeping," she whispered, and somehow the whisper was worse than a scream.

Anne squeezed her eyes shut, shaking her head.

Sometimes, if she were honest, she wished Rachel could just disappear for good. It would be safer, better for them all without the wicked girl.

Wicked girl. Wretched girl. Cursed girl.

Chapter Six
Candace

Her head spinning, Candace climbed under the welcoming comforter on her bed and slowly inhaled the scent of the familiar floral laundry detergent. The only light peeked in from the moon through the blinds, casting odd shadows about her. She closed her eyes, the strangeness of the bed feeling somehow familiar, too, as she started to drift to sleep. Exhaustion weighed heavily on her, each limb pressed down into the soft sheets. Still, the weightlessness of dreamland didn't come right away.

She couldn't get those images out of her mind. What had they been? The more she tried to shove them aside, the more they rose up from her subconscious, drowning her brain in creepy pictures of scissors, of red, of scratched walls, of long black hair. Queasiness gurgled in her stomach.

It's the wine, she told herself again, imploring her mind to quiet. It was just a fantastical day, that was all. An odd juxtaposition of the past and present, with Grandma Anne's decorations on the tree, with her old friends stopping by, with the very real event of going to bed alone, again. Always alone.

She finally drifted off, but thoughts of Landon leaving plagued her. At least those bad memories pushed down the confusing images that made her stomach roil.

HER HEART ACHED AS she sat straight up, confusion rocking her as her eyes peeled open. She squeezed her hands into fists as she quickly assessed the room, remembering first that she wasn't in New York anymore. Remembering slowly where she was. And then, with a chill, remembering what had awakened her.

A crash. From the kitchen. Someone was inside.

She felt the panicked teenager within her rise up as she reached under the bed for the trustworthy baseball bat. She stowed one under every bed in the house, including the guest bedroom. It was thankfully still there. Growing up, she'd begged her mother to let her hide a handgun in every room, but she'd forbidden it. She'd told Candance that she didn't need to worry, that Marian would protect her. Well, where was Marian now?

Candace waited a long moment, holding in her breath so she could listen. Nothing. Stillness. But wasn't that what happened in all the movies?

She wasn't fifteen anymore. She was twenty-six. Brave. Fearless. Or so she told herself. She wouldn't sit there waiting to be murdered. Her head ached from the wine, but she tiptoed out of bed, careful to avoid the creaky board by the dresser. She creeped to the door, cracking it open so slowly it was painful.

She steadied her breath, baseball bat in her left hand as she edged down the hallway.

Her mother's bedroom was upstairs, and Grandma Anne's—Candace's old bedroom—was on the other side of the house. It was just her down here, alone, nothing but a bathroom and an office to protect her. She inched down the hallway, feeling like she was in one of the movies she would've screamed at. What was she doing? She should've called 911. She should've texted her mother. Anything. Something. But it was too late to turn back.

There was some scuttling in the kitchen, some scratching noises. Candance, never the patient one, walked faster toward the noise. Better to face up to her fate. If she was a dead woman, so be it. She turned the corner—and just before she swung her bat into the brains of the burglar, her heart racing . . .

She sighed in relief, laughing to herself as she shook her head.

Muffin, all fifteen pounds of him, sat in the middle of the kitchen, a broken glass scattered about him.

"Stupid cat," she murmured, grabbing a paper towel to sweep the pieces up haphazardly and throw them in the trash.

She set the bat down on the counter, carefully picking up the glass so as to not wake her mother or grandmother. Although she would be talking with her mother the next day. All those years she assured Candace she was safe, that she would protect her—turned out Marian was a deep sleeper. Too deep of a sleeper to even hear the deafening crash from an overweight cat's antics.

Once the glass was semi-cleaned up, Candance walked back toward her bedroom. She stopped, though, for a moment, peering into the living room at the tree. Mom hadn't turned off the lights. Odd. Her mother was always paranoid about fires, understandably. In truth, she was always paranoid about everything. Candace sighed, her head still throbbing. She considered heading straight to the bathroom for Tylenol, but the image of the house up in flames freaked her out too much. She headed to the tree to unplug the lights. She reached for the cord, yanking it as Muffin, now meowing at her feet, rubbed her legs and almost tripped her.

She was turning to head back to her bedroom when the ornament caught her eye.

One too many.

What the hell did that mean? Was it some Christmas carol from the past? She'd have to google it in the morning. Curiosity stirred within. She reached for the ornament, wanting to touch it, to see if it would happen again. But she was afraid.

She pulled her hand back, scolding herself for being ridiculous. Still, she couldn't bring herself to touch it. She headed to the bathroom, took a small pill to ease her headache, and crawled back into bed. Just as she was drifting back to her broken dreams, though, her heart beat crazily again, her skin clammy.

The images flashed. Red. Scissors. The girl . . .

And then, before the images could finish circling in her mind, footsteps. Loud, stomping footsteps in her room. Unmistakable.

She'd been right. He was here. He'd broken in, and—in a panic, she thrust herself over the bed, reaching for the bat. She remembered too late that it was in the kitchen. The footsteps stomped to the other side of her room and then seemed to come closer. Slower now. She scuttled back against the wall, ready to scream as she faced her fate. It was only then she realized—her door was still closed. She hadn't heard it open. Had she? She turned to the dresser, looking into the mirror. Before the scream echoed through the house, before her piercing cries woke even her deep sleeping mother, Candance saw the image that wouldn't stop haunting her.

The girl. The black-haired girl, scissors in her hand. Covered in scratches and blood, she peered at Candace, smiling way too wide with way too perfect teeth. And as her scream echoed, as her mother dashed to her room to see what was wrong, Candace heard the scratchy words before the girl disappeared.

"One too many," she whispered, and it was unmistakable that Candace had stirred something dark when she'd plucked that unassuming box from the attic.

Chapter Seven
Marian

Marian Mills knew the wine had been a bad idea. What had she been thinking? She *was* a bad mother, after all, her greatest fear coming to fruition.

The familiar sentiment crept in as it had so many times over the decades as Marian put on a pot of coffee. Her head ached from the alcohol and from the terrors of the night, when she'd heard Candace's scream. Of course, her mind had instantly gone to him. Even after all these years, he had that kind of pull on them all. She'd grabbed the handgun from her nightstand, dashing toward the scream.

It had been a nightmare. Only a nightmare. Still, she hadn't sighed in relief when she saw her daughter pressed against the wall screaming about footsteps and the ornament. She'd comforted Candace like she had when she was young, when the nightmares first started. After the incident. After the world turned upside down. After Marian realized she could never earn the title of good mother, no matter how hard she tried. She'd brought him into their lives, after all. She'd done that to her daughter.

Even now that Candace was all grown up, she couldn't help but worry. She hated that her daughter had moved to the city, so far out of reach. She knew that Candace had struggled with alcohol before. Why had she served the wine? Stupid mother. Stupid woman. Stupid altogether.

Marian heard her own mother's soft snoring down the hall. Grandma Anne had been alarmed at the screams, but had gone back to sleep, mercifully. At least she didn't have one of her episodes as well. Still, it had been grating on the nerves, settling Candace back in, assuring her it was just her throttled brain and the stress of travelling, that there was nothing to worry about.

Marian poured herself a cup of coffee, jaunting over to the tiny table to sit like she always did in the morning. Two days until Christmas. She'd always hated this time of year, the stress of trying to provide a happy moment for Candace when money was never plentiful. Still, she'd managed, somehow, every year. At least this year, they were together. At least this year, maybe they could create some new memories.

Marian glanced into the living room then, looking at the tree. The lights were plugged in. Marian knew she'd unplugged them last night. Had Candace or Anne plugged them in during the night? Peculiar. She'd have to ask them. She set down her steaming cup of Folger's, her slippers trudging to the tree to unplug the lights. She always hated leaving them plugged in, afraid of a faulty outlet on the old house. As she approached the fake evergreen, they flickered, as if to say, "See, it isn't safe."

A chill brushed through her, but Marian just blamed the aging furnace, the biting temperature in the rickety house a common ordeal. She pulled her robe tighter as she leaned down to unplug the lights which were flickering more intensely now. She'd have to tell Anne and Candace to leave them unplugged. The tree would have to suffice without the lights. She was heading back to her coffee, needing to sit and just prepare for what to-do lists she needed to check off today when her eyes landed on it.

The bell. She squeezed her eyes shut against the memories of the images. The scissors. The odd-looking girl. The surge and the horrifying dread that filled her veins when she'd touched it. The ornament gave her the creeps. She wished Candace had just left it in the attic. It clearly had stirred something in Anne, too, the way her eyes got all faraway looking and how it had incited her eerie chanting. And there had been the zap, the images. What the hell happened?

She sighed, knowing it was the stress of the holidays. She needed to make this Christmas perfect, as perfect as it could be. Maybe if she showed Candace how important family was, how good it could be to be surrounded by love, she'd change her mind about that cold city she lived in. She'd stop pretending that spreading her wings was the right choice, and she'd come home. Where she belonged. Where Marian could keep her safe.

Marian headed back to the kitchen to enjoy a few more peaceful moments before the family woke up. As she was stepping away from the tree, she paused and listened.

It was a faint whisper, almost too quiet to be real. And as she listened harder, leaning toward the tree despite her body screaming to get away, she assured herself it must just be the wind outside or her sleepy imagination or the craziness from last night. But Marian couldn't shove the words aside, the same words Candace was chanting through her tears last night.

One too many.

What the hell was going on in this place? She brushed the question aside as she headed back to her steaming mug, taking a long swallow as she thought about how thankful she was that the gun was always loaded nearby.

Chapter Eight
Candace

The old-timey Christmas song blared through the countertop radio as Candace sealed the envelope, her fingers aching from all the writing.

"I don't know why we're even doing this. It's almost Christmas. People won't get them until after the holidays."

"It's tradition," her mother replied curtly, scrawling the name of a distant cousin carefully on the front of the envelope she was working on.

Candace took a break, sipping from her mug of hot chocolate. All the years she'd participated in this tradition came flooding back. Sitting here with her mother, the tree in the corner of the living room as the same songs played. Her mother never had a lot, but she'd always tried to make Christmas special. And she'd always insisted on sending Christmas cards, even when Candace knew they could barely make the mortgage payment.

Candace worked on the remaining cards in her pile silently. Her mother hadn't mentioned last night at all, and Candace was glad. She didn't need a Marian interrogation about her drinking or if the nightmares were back. She just needed to put it behind her. Time ticked by, and Candace was actually enjoying the peace. Her mother was just telling her about a visit she was planning to see cousin Julie when the tranquility was shattered by Grandma Anne's screams. Candace and Marian dashed back the hallway toward the noise.

"She's probably having one of her spells," Marian warned as they crashed through the bedroom door where Grandma Anne had been taking a nap. But when they got to the room, it was very clear that this spell was different.

Grandma Anne was sobbing and shaking in the corner of her room. How the woman who could barely hobble about managed to get to the floor was the first oddity of the scene but not the worst. Candace shrieked as she saw the blood trickling down her grandmother's arms.

"Mom, calm down, calm down," Marian begged, approaching the screaming woman. Grandma Anne looked right past Marian, into the corner of the room. Candace turned, a knot in her stomach. And as Marian calmed down Grandma Anne, helping her up and examining the slices on her arms, Candace was sure it wasn't wine or hot cocoa or anything else this time.

Because in the corner of the room, where Grandma Anne's eyes were fixated, Candace saw the black-haired girl who had haunted her last night. This time, though, was different. In the somber girl's hands were a pair of rusty scissors dripping with blood.

The next shriek wasn't Anne's. It was Candace's as she realized this was a much bigger problem than she could've ever imagined.

"WICKED GIRL, WICKED girl," Grandma Anne murmured in her chair in the living room. Her chants were rhythmic, slobber dripping down the old woman's chin as she muttered on and on and on. She was a broken record shattered by the horrors Marian and Candace were only beginning to unearth. Marian had cleaned up the cuts on the woman's pale skin, chattering on and on about how she had no idea how the woman had managed to hurt herself so badly.

"Poor thing just gets so confused sometimes," Marian murmured, but Candace didn't say a word. She was staring at the tree, at the ornament, wondering how it had all come together like this and, more importantly, why.

"She's back. She's going to kill us all," Grandma Anne said now, her unsteady eyes red and tear-filled. "Please, we need to get out. She's going to kill us."

"Mom, it's okay, calm down," Marian reassured her. She approached the woman who was staring, trance-like, at the corner of the room. Candace chilled to the core, her eyes following her Grandma's line of sight. This time, she saw nothing. She exhaled a breath she didn't realize she'd been holding.

"I wonder if I should call the doctor," Marian whispered to Candace.

Candace looked up into her mother's face. What the hell was happening? How could she explain . . . were they all going mad? But as Marian walked to get the cordless phone, Candace grabbed her arm with an icy hand.

"Mom, she's not crazy. I saw it too." The words tumbled out, burning her raw throat on the way out.

Marian stopped, looking at her daughter. "What? Saw what?"

"Her. The black-haired girl. She was in Grandma's room."

"What?" Marian asked again, and Candace saw a look that suggested maybe she had gone mad. Candace took a deep breath. Grandma Anne quieted, perhaps relieved that someone believed her.

"It was the same girl who I saw. But. . ." Candace paused. It was ludicrous. How could she even suggest . . . but she saw it. She saw the girl, haunting and eerie, with the evil grin on her face. She saw the cuts on Grandma Anne's arm, saw the blood dripping down.

"What? Tell me."

"She had scissors." Candace's muscles tightened at the word, at the sight. The unsettling image of the girl crouched nearby with scissors in her hand—scissors she clearly intended to do harm with. It was madness, truly—but it was real, Candace admitted. There was no other explanation.

Tears pooled and blurred her vision, but Marian shook her head. "What? It makes no sense."

"She's back," Grandma Anne announced, interrupting their conversation. She had calmed to a slow rock now in her chair, her eyes lasered on the tree. Her words were stoic and pointed, the slobber wiped from her chin. Clarity settled into the woman's pale eyes, clarity that couldn't even be disturbed by the woman's cloudy cataracts or failing eyesight.

"Mom, who is back?" Marian asked, a tremble in her voice.

"Rachel. She's back. And she's going to make me pay."

Chapter Nine
Anne
1955

Anne sat on her bed, staring out the frost-covered window of the bedroom she shared with her sister. Rachel's black braided hair whipped in the wind, her body shaking as she pressed her face against the window. Anne could see the tears falling down, cascading into the glass. She wondered if Rachel would freeze to the window, die of hypothermia in her short-sleeved dress Mother had thrown her outside in.

Anne rocked back and forth, staring into the eyes of her pitiful twin sister. A piece of her rose up and felt sorry for her, freezing in the backyard as Mother ranted on the phone in the hallway. Dad would never handle Rachel this way. He always had a more sympathetic heart, even when Rachel was being reckless. But Mother religiously let Rachel know how she felt.

"That girl is out of control, Mom," Anne's mother screamed into the phone, talking to their grandma who lived in Philadelphia. "I can't take it anymore. I'm ready to send her back to Redwood or to a convent."

Anne bit her lip, listening in. Her mother's voice raised in agitation now.

"I know, Mother. I know I can't send her back there or our reputation will be ruined for good. But it will be anyway if I don't do something, the way that girl is acting. There are so many rumors circulating already. It isn't fair to Anne that our family gets this reputation because of Rachel's demented actions. Anne is going to be looking for a nice boy to marry soon. What will her chances be with Rachel's behavior? No one is going to want to touch this family with a ten-foot pole."

Anne rotated from the window, turning her back on her crying sister. Mother was right. Rachel's actions were ridiculous and selfish. Anne had worked so hard in school to keep her reputation golden. She wanted to marry a nice man, settle in the suburbs, and have the kind of life she deserved.

Rachel was going to spoil all of that. There were rules for appropriate behavior. And sure, Rachel had always been a little different. Had always been trouble. But they were past the years of irresponsible behaviors melting away. They were at the crossroads in their lives, where actions would lead to life-altering consequences.

"I don't know how they're twins. I honestly forget sometimes because they're so different. Anne is just so picture-perfect, sweet. She brings pride to the family while Rachel brings nothing but shame," her mother continued.

Anne didn't have to listen to hear the next statement. About how Rachel had been the unwanted one. How her mother hadn't known she was having twins until after Anne had been birthed and the doctor shared the so-called great news. There was a second baby, Rachel. A twin, a friend, a blessing for Anne. Rachel had been anything but, and Mother often reminded her that she wasn't what they'd wanted. Sometimes Anne thought maybe her mother's harsh words had worn on Rachel's brain, had made her act differently.

There was a thudding on the glass now. Anne turned. Rachel was pounding her head against the window, gaping blankly at her. First, it was a soft thudding, and Anne was annoyed. But then, the hammering intensified. Louder and louder, the window rattled with the impact. Anne stood up, alarmed.

"Stop that!" Anne shouted, watching as the snow cascaded down, as Rachel clunked her head over and over, her soulless stare never leaving Anne.

"Stop!" she shrieked again. She was going to crack the window, crack her skull. Hadn't she caused enough trouble today?

Abandoning the phone, Mother padded down the hallway. "What's going on?" she asked, storming into the room. She glanced at the peeling frame on the window, running toward the scene.

"Rachel, enough!" Mother squealed as Anne shriveled back, not wanting to handle any more of it.

It was supposed to be a fun night out for milkshakes, a chance for Rachel to prove that she could be normal. The girls had gone on a double date with the Archie twins, Robert and Anthony. Rachel had been paired with Robert, the quieter of the two. She hadn't wanted to go, begged her mother not to make her go with the nerdy boy who referred to Rachel as the psycho in town. Mother had insisted that Rachel had gotten the bad reputation through her countless acts—murdering the Clinton's cat last fall, painting a red cross on the Felton's garage when they'd called Rachel's outfit unholy, swearing at every teacher at the school. Rachel needed redemption, Mother had said. Rachel found a way to her own form of redemption, a darker kind.

The night had gone well at first, Rachel silently chewing on her fries as Robert mumbled on and on about politics and things no one cared about. Anne smiled and played the role of the admirable female, doting and polite. Rachel had stared into her plate blankly. The two Archie boys had exchanged glances.

"We heard you were choked in the womb," Robert said to Rachel. "I mean, obviously Anne is the normal one."

Anne stopped eating, bile rising in her throat. Rachel wasn't a good person, and there had been many wrongs done to Anne over the years. Still, she was her twin, her sister. Didn't she owe it to her out of familial love to protect her?

"Robert," Anne murmured. Rachel, though, had sunk into herself, into that dark part of herself where even Anne couldn't reach her. The girl let her black braids fall into her face. Her hands shaking, she reached for the fork.

And before Robert could respond or make a lame joke, before Anne could attempt to talk sense into her sister, no matter how pointless, Rachel had jabbed the fork with a downward thrust into the boy's hand. The shriek, the expletives, the general confusion that followed as blood streamed and the manager rushed out didn't shake Rachel.

She stared straight ahead, a blankness in her.

Perhaps that was the scariest part of her. Not the evil lurking beneath the surface, not the crude acts of hostility. No, for Anne, the most horrifying part about her sister was in her apathetic response to danger, to everything. It was like Rachel was gone, dead inside. It was like she was born without something—empathy? Compassion? A soul?

Mother had been called, and there were the typical pleasantries and discussions about how hastily Rachel had acted, the apologies. The smiles. There had been the car ride home with Mother berating Rachel, threatening to send her back again to that place Rachel did not like to speak of. It was the only thing that brought her out of her shell, the threats of sending her back. It incited the girl to become the shouting, hate-filled creature Anne shied away from. There had been a night ruined, reputations ruined, promises that Rachel would be sent away if there was one more outburst.

"Rachel, I'm not kidding. You psychotic slut, stop it! I've had it. Can't you see what you're doing to this family? Do you want us to send you back to that place?" Mother shouted, bringing Anne back to the present trauma of the window. With Rachel, there was always a trauma, always something else.

Rachel's face was set in a slight grin. When she committed evil acts that hurt others, like the fork in Robert's hand, she was blank. But when Rachel did things that frightened Mother, Anne always detected the hint of malice mixing with joy. Rachel wanted Mother to pay.

Anne shook away the creeping feelings. Rachel was still smashing her head against the glass, Mother now pounding back on the window. It was like a game, seeing who would crack it first.

"Let her in, Mother. Maybe we should let her in. It's freezing outside," Anne begged, wanting the deafening noise, the harrowing tension to stop, just for a moment.

"Good. Maybe we'll freeze the devil out of her. Jesus, Anne, how can you defend her?"

"I'm not. Trust me, I'm not." And she wasn't. Anne knew her sister was a monster. Mother was right. Rachel was one too many.

She had to be stopped before she ruined them for good. The town was probably abuzz with Rachel's latest stunt. It was all anyone would be talking about on Monday, and Anne would have to cover it up, play the mediator. She was tired of protecting the beast who was still thrusting herself at the window.

Mother slapped the glass again. "Stop it, you devil. You devil. You shouldn't have been born. We'd have been better off if you were never born."

Mother was trembling, tears falling. She grabbed the vase that was on Anne's desk and hurled it at the window. The glass shattered, the vase flying through and just missing Rachel's head. The girl didn't move, staring straight through. But she wasn't staring at her mother. Her eyes were still locked on Anne. And wordlessly, it was like she was telling her all she needed to know. There would be a next time. And it wouldn't be Robert's hand spewing blood.

There had been so many nights when Anne awoke to find Rachel standing over her, glowering. "The pretty twin," she whispered. "Everyone loves you. But you're no better than me." Anne had difficulty returning to sleep, even after Rachel had returned to her side of the room.

There had always been the little things, too, over the years. Missing items. Dolls with their heads pulled off. A tack in Anne's bed. But now that they were older, the stakes were growing. And Rachel was getting more violent.

"Stand up for me, Sister," Rachel had begged her last week when their mother was on a tirade about Rachel. "Don't you see how she treats me?"

"You deserve it," Anne had replied, spewing back the words her mother had taught her as gospel. Rachel deserved what she

got. She'd made her bed, ever since she was little. Anne was good and kind. She followed the rules, greeted everyone with niceties. She obeyed her parents and got good grades. Rachel was Rachel. There was no changing that.

Their mother stormed out of the room, and Rachel stood frozen in the swirl of snow, the remnants of the broken window all around her. Anne knew when their father got home, he'd hear about the date gone wrong. Their mother would tell him that Rachel had broken the window. And no matter how much Rachel pleaded, he'd believe her. Because Anne would agree. She always did. If she had to pick a side, after all, it was smarter to pick Mother's side. Rachel was dangerous. Rachel needed to pay. And even if Dad couldn't see it, Rachel needed to be sent away for all of their sakes. Why couldn't he see it?

Rachel's eyes stared at Anne, and she felt a pang of guilt. This was her sister. What must it be like to be her? What pain must she be in? Still, Anne shoved it aside, knowing the dangers of commiserating with the enemy. Anne turned and walked away, leaving Rachel alone in the cold, lost and forgotten just like she deserved.

Her mother was right. Rachel was the bad seed. She needed to disappear. It would all be better if that horrific girl with the dark ideas just went away for good.

Chapter Ten
Marian

Marian had never been a superstitious woman. She opened umbrellas inside—easier than getting all wet outside struggling to get the stupid thing open. She walked by black cats without blinking an eye, and breaking a mirror didn't bring her any worse luck than before. She had settled into a life as a realist. True, she tried her best to be optimistic. You had to when you were a single mother, after all. But she was grounded in reality, and her feet were firmly planted on the dusty ground where they belonged. There were enough scary things in the real world. She didn't need to go believing old wives' tales or ghost stories.

Nevertheless, there was no denying it. Something bizarre was at work in their tiny house at 1119 Maple Street. Somehow, the trees that once felt like a line of protection and privacy around the house felt like a cave of doom. The sky felt a little too dark above the house, the rooms a little dingier. And if she closed her eyes, it was as if she could smell a tinge of rusty copper and death floating in the air. Things were definitely off in the house.

She wanted to attribute it to the stress of the holidays. She'd tried blaming Candance's mental condition and her mother's. She'd blamed the alcohol. But there was no mitigating it. They'd all experienced the inexplicable. They'd all seen the blood dripping down Anne's arm, witnessed the sense of dread they felt near the ornament, near the tree. And now, they had to fix it. Fear was just a feeling, after all. It could be stopped, just like anything else if you were willing to find the solution.

After she brushed aside the doubts and oozing terror within, she did what she always did. She took charge of the situation. She'd cleaned up the mess. She'd calmed her mother down, getting her on her favorite topic—*The Price is Right*. She'd sent Candace to get a pizza for dinner to keep her busy and get her out of the house. She'd calmed everyone down, reassured them that it would be fine, even as Anne periodically asked if Rachel was back.

Marian took a deep breath. She'd of course known about her deceased aunt, her mother's twin sister. She'd seen a picture once from when they were little girls. The moody, dark child look troubled even at the age of five. But Anne didn't talk about her sister. It seemed to trouble her mother when the name Rachel was even brought up. So Rachel had been tucked away in the past, where she apparently belonged.

Yet here they were, facing the terrors from what Anne believed was Rachel. Impossible. The girl had been dead for how many decades now? Why would this be happening? And what would Rachel possibly want with them? Ghosts weren't real, Marian knew. The real monsters walked the earth in human flesh. Everything had an explanation, and certainly this did, too.

Still, there had been the blood, and her daughter's insistence of what she saw. It was insane. This wasn't a Stephen King novel. It was real life. Still, as Marian dried her hands on the towel after washing dishes, her favorite thing to do when she felt like she was losing her mind, she wandered back to the living room and stared.

The ornament. The Christmas bell. Hadn't it all started then? Hadn't Marian felt that initial shock with her own hands, seen the vivid images that were terrifying and confusing? It seemed like some kind of fantastical explanation, but at this point, Marian was willing to try anything. She just wanted to finish out the holiday with peace and happiness. She wouldn't let anything ruin it.

So she did what she needed to do. Without hesitation, she grabbed the garbage can. Couldn't be too careful after all. She trudged to the tree, eyeing the rusty red bell with the eerie scratchings. It certainly looked possessed, if nothing else. Taking a deep breath, she batted it off the tree, a jolt pulsing through her as she touched it. She could only describe it as a surge of odd energy, a heat coupled with a stomach-dropping sensation. A flash of red, of blood, of scissors came into her head, but she didn't pause to reflect. *Enough of this weird shit,* she thought.

She rushed out the front door with the garbage can, passing the junk drawer in the kitchen on the way. She grabbed the lighter from her early days of bad habits and bingeing, carrying it with her.

In the backyard, she set the trash can down, flicked the lighter, and lit the contents on fire. It seemed a bit like overkill, but she didn't really know the protocol for dealing with a potentially demonic ornament. Fire seemed like the best solution, even though it stirred an eerie sensation in the pit of her stomach. It was fine, she was in control. Fire wouldn't kill her, not last time, not this time. But maybe it would kill whatever was going on in that ornament. She watched the flames and the smoke billow, exhaled a breath she didn't know she was holding, and walked over to get the hose to put the fire out.

She peeked in the trash can, seeing the now charred Christmas ornament at the bottom. Marian rolled her eyes at her own ridiculous behavior. The thing was metal. What had she expected to accomplish with her little sanctimonious fire? She shook her head, setting the can into the bigger can by the curb. It was garbage night tonight. They would say goodbye to that weird little ornament and whatever was tied to it. They would enjoy the rest of the Christmas season, happy together. Just like they should be.

She rubbed her hands on the front of her pants, wiping them clean of the bizarre occurrences of the past few days. It was nothing she couldn't handle. Marian, after all, had handled everything life had thrown at her. She'd cleaned it all up and carried Candace through, making sure she wasn't scorned or scarred. Hadn't she?

She wandered back inside, thinking about what Christmas movie they'd watch after dinner. Glancing at the clock, she figured Candace should be home any minute. What was taking her so long to get a pizza?

Inefficient. She loved her daughter, but the girl was scattered. Marian dug out some paper plates, setting the table before going to her mother's bedroom. Her mother was sleeping peacefully, a small smile on her face. See? It was all going to be just fine.

But when Marian walked back down the hallway, her eyes stopped as she got to the living room entrance. The tree was alight, the twinkling lights blinking in a haphazard way. Her stomach roiled, and then it plummeted as if she were careening off a cliff to her ultimate demise. Maybe she was. For as Marian crept closer to the tree, her hands started to shake.

She wasn't a superstitious woman. She didn't believe in ghosts or old wives' tales.

But how could anyone in the real world explain how the hell the Christmas bell that she'd just set on fire and then put out for the trash was now hanging right where it was, gleaming as though it had never been touched? It swayed softly on the branch, calling attention to itself. And just as Grandma Anne yelled for Marian, just as Marian prepared to shriek, the door to the house flew open.

"Mom?" Candace's voice bellowed. "Mom, we have a major problem. We're in trouble," her voice resonated, quaking with terror that Marian felt within her core.

They *were* in trouble. Marian might be able to handle the situation with Joe. She might be able to protect her daughter from that monster. But how would she protect them from an enemy unseen?

Chapter Eleven
Candace

The steaming pizza on the front seat beside her, Candace breathed in the scent of salt, sauce, and cheese. Her mother had tried to assuage the situation with food as she often did. However, Candace wasn't a child anymore. She could see right through Marian's ridiculous attempts to brush this craziness aside. She wished it could be that easy.

Candace's head pounded worse than when she was hungover. Coming home for Christmas no longer seemed like such a wonderful idea. It seemed like a curse. Her mind fluttered back to times from her past, other dark times when things seemed surreal and uncontainable. Her chest tightened, thinking about the constant feeling of danger, of her mother trying to reassure her with pizza.

She knew then that things weren't okay. She knew it from the gun underneath her mother's pillow, from her constant vigilance, from the overly enthusiastic smile that looked so fake on her face. Candace could see through her mother's painted-on sense of calmness and bravery then. She could see through it now, too.

Candace pulled out of the parking lot, deciding she wasn't ready to go home just yet. The pizza could cool for a while. Not like anyone but Grandma Anne would have an appetite, and even that was questionable. She pulled into the parking lot, parked the car, and ambled inside the local grocery, deciding to get some dessert and salad to add to the already pointless meal.

It seemed even more outrageous, waltzing down the aisles examining lettuce leaves when there was a potential haunting, a wicked girl from Grandma's past, creeping through the house. Candace examined the organic lettuce and wondered if it really was any different than the regular. Her mind just needed to focus on something else, something she could control.

"Candace?" a soft voice whispered, and she jumped, lettuce leaves in hand. Turning slowly, she breathed a sigh of relief when it was just Eva standing behind a cart.

"Hey, how are you?" Candace said too quickly. She could feel the inherited fake smile painting itself on.

Eva, usually bubbly, bit her lip and tucked a strand of hair behind her ear. Now that Candace looked at her, she didn't look good. Bags under her eyes, gray skin. Maybe she was just working a lot of overtime. Still, she'd changed so much since last night. Had it really only been last night that all hell had broken loose?

"O-okay," Eva stammered, staring at the floor.

"You sure?" she asked, stepping closer as Eva took a step back.

There was a long pause, and Candace wondered if this was how they would part, both going their separate ways down produce aisles, wishing a faint-hearted Merry Christmas to each other from across the store. But then, Eva seemed to get a hold of herself. She took a step forward, whispering so that Candace had to lean in.

"Um, has anything—strange happened to you? Since last night?"

Candace met Eva's eyes, and her stomach started to churn. She felt hot and cold at the same time, her brain jumping to wild conclusions. She told herself to breathe as she set the lettuce back.

"What kind of things?" she asked, her voice hissing.

Eva tucked another strand behind her ear. "Things. I don't know. Strange things. Since—the ornament. Since—the images."

The scissors. Rachel. The red. So Eva had seen it too.

"A black-haired girl?" Candace asked, each word articulated like it was a witch's spell.

Eva nodded solemnly. "Pat thinks I've lost it. He thinks it's all the hours on the job. But I know what I saw. It wasn't a nightmare."

Tears welled in her eyes, her hands shaking. She leaned on the cart as if to steady herself. Candace stepped forward.

"I saw her too. You're not crazy. You're not crazy at all." Candace was now trembling, iciness freezing the blood in her veins. There was no denying it. No matter how fantastical or wickedly weird it all was, one thing was for sure. It was real. It was all real.

"What was that ornament? What was it?" Eva's voice raised now, and Candace shushed her, looking to see if they were drawing attention to themselves. Wouldn't do to get them all locked up when the town assumed they had all lost it.

"We don't know," Candace admitted honestly. "We think it has something to do with Grandma."

"Candace, what are we going to do?" Eva looked at Candace imploringly. Growing up, Eva had been the strong, wily one. The one up for adventure. Now, she was looking to Candace to be the strength, to have the answers.

"I don't know. I really don't know. But I don't think this is about you. It's about Grandma. So stay calm. I'm sure it's going to be fine."

Eva nodded, hanging onto every word, perhaps needing to believe Candace was right. She swiped at her tears. "Be safe," she said.

Candace didn't know what else to do. She hugged Eva, and then walked away. There was, after all, no reconciling for something like this. Any apology would be weak and underdone.

Candace abandoned her empty shopping basket in the aisle, ready to head home. Needing to head home, to tell her mother that things were worse than they thought. Marian would know what to do, wouldn't she? She'd fixed so many things before. A broken bicycle. A scarred knee. A ruined prom night. A dangerous ex. Surely Marian would figure this out, too. No one died from a ghost anyway. So this spirit was haunting them. They'd get an exorcist or make an offering or destroy the ornament and it would be fine. Happy holidays. Case closed. But as she was heading to the exit, Candace turned around, a thought striking her.

"Eva?" she called across the store. Eva paused, tensing. She turned to look at Candace.

"Have you talked to Rosalie?"

Eva shook her head no. "Not since last night." She shuddered at the memory, perhaps involuntarily.

Candace took a deep breath. Okay. So they would need to talk to Rosalie, to see if she had any more information. Maybe together they could piece it together, figure out what this ghost wanted, make it go away. She reassured herself on the way out of the grocery store, hopping into the car. But on the ten-minute drive home, her heart began to race. Her breathing quickened. Because as she put distance between herself and the grocery store, heading home to the unknown, she knew that it wasn't okay. Nothing about this was okay. And then, after parking in the driveway, leaning to get the pizza, her eyes glanced into the rearview mirror.

The black hair, the blood-stained cheeks. Candace screamed. It definitely wasn't fucking okay.

"MOM, WE HAVE A MAJOR problem. We're in trouble," Candace bellowed as she stormed through the door, winded. She'd left the pizza in the car, not caring about the extra cheese pie with that demon in the car.

She expected her mother to come rushing as she always did, to help make things better. Where would she begin? The whole thing with Eva, the backseat view—but as she took inventory of the house as she walked in, she realized the problems were just beginning.

Her mother was standing at the tree, staring at the ornament. In the background, Candace heard her grandmother yelling, too. The house was chaos, and for once, Marian stood, frozen, as if she didn't know what to do.

"Mom?"

Marian turned to face her. Candace noticed her mother's skin was gray and pallid, as if she were ready to drop over dead.

"Marian," Anne's voice screeched again. Candace took a breath, following her mother back the hallway.

"She's here. She's here. She's here," Anne chanted, cradling herself, rocking. "The wicked girl is here. She's going to take us all. She's going to kill us all."

"Mom, calm down," Marian whispered, but Candace knew at this point, it was useless. There was no calming down.

"Everyone take a breath," Marian ordered. "It's going to be okay."

"It's not," Candace yelled. "It's not okay. Eva saw her too."

"What?" Grandma Anne asked. "She saw Rachel?"

"Shit," Marian exclaimed before Candace told her mother all about the grocery store, about the car. Marian exchanged stories, telling of the ornament.

The whole time, Grandma Anne rocked, saying "wicked girl" over and over, adding to Candace's already pounding headache. It was a damn mess. Candace wanted nothing more than to pack up her car and go back to New York City where she belonged, where the biggest fear was how to afford rent.

"What are we going to do?" she asked, her lip quivering as she sat on her grandmother's bed beside her mother.

"We're going to sort it out," Marian replied, but Candace noticed her mother's voice was shaky. And for the first time in her life, Candace thought she witnessed a tear rolling down her mother's cheek.

"Kill Rachel. Kill her again," Grandma Anne whispered into the darkness, and both women turned to look at the elderly woman who had a fire burning in her eyes that wasn't there before.

"Again?" Candace mouthed, the words not even audible.

Grandma Anne turned to her granddaughter, her eyes piercing through her. "She deserved it. She's a wicked girl."

And Candace's stomach dropped as she began to wonder what secrets the family was harboring after all.

Chapter Twelve
Marian

They needed to examine the scope of this thing, to understand just how far the reach of it was before they could get a handle on it. There would be time to discuss options—exorcisms, séances, whatever the hell you did in these scenarios. Marian thought there was a Ouija board in the attic. But first thing was first. They needed to call Rosalie, to see if she was experiencing it, too.

Candace sighed, picking up her phone to call again. They'd been calling for hours to no avail. Sure, time had distanced her daughter from her good friend, but this wasn't like Rosalie. That girl was always glued to her phone.

"No luck. Mom, this is ridiculous. What good will this do?"

"We need to sort this out the right way. I need to know if she's seeing the stuff too. It could help us figure out what Rachel wants."

Marian rolled her eyes at herself, hating that the being, the experience, the inexplicable was now being referred to as Rachel, as if she were just another person in their lives. She'd asked questions of Anne, but her mother clammed up at the mere mention of her twin sister. Marian didn't know if it was the dementia confusing her, or if there was something dark that Anne didn't want to talk about. Regardless, they'd cross that bridge with time. One item on the list at a time. That's how you got something done.

"Listen, I think we need to go over there," Marian said.

"Mom, really. Don't we have bigger issues?"

"We can't tackle this thing until we know all the details," Marian replied calmly, taking a sip of water. "You can stay with Grandma. I'll go."

"And what are you going to say? Hey, are you seeing a creepy fucking ghost from the past?"

"We know Eva saw her too. It's not ridiculous. I just want to check on her. She's alone, after all. We need to make sure she's okay. We have a responsibility to make sure she's okay."

Candace's face grew grim. She hadn't wanted to scare her daughter, but they needed to get real. Things had escalated quickly. Who knew what kind of danger they could be in?

HER KNUCKLES WERE SORE from rapping, and her chest was heavy with an inexplicable sense of dread. There were moments in her life that Marian knew something dark was coming just before it happened. Maybe it was just in the air. Maybe she had a sixth sense for disaster because she'd lived through the whole situation with Joe. Or maybe it was just the fact that the air felt marred with melancholy.

"Rosalie? It's me, Ms. Mills. I need to talk to you," she yelled again, but there was no response. The logical thing would be to leave, to come back later, but she needed answers. And she needed to see if her intuition was right.

So she turned the doorknob—and found it unlocked. The heavy white door creaked open, and Marian inched in slowly, trying to stay concealed. Her heart pounded, and her nose inhaled an odd, metallic scent that just didn't seem right.

"Rosalie?" she said again, hesitantly, almost choking on the name.

She heard a rustle from a back room, a whisper. Was it a whisper? Marian wished she wasn't alone. She inched forward, down the hallway in the unfamiliar house that only jarred her nerves more. She creeped along, not knowing what she expected to find, convincing herself she was being crazy.

But as she followed the whispered murmurs, wondering if Rosalie needed help, she stopped outside what appeared to be a bedroom door. The metallic scent was stronger, and the whispers were louder. They surged in intensity, and Marian covered her ears. A muffled giggle swept through her, but the tone was off.

Her hands shook, pressed to her ears. She should call the police. She should get out of there—but curiosity got the better of her. And her mothering instincts. What if Rosalie needed her? She couldn't leave. Still, the whispers and giggling louder now, she could make out what the eerie words were.

"It's your turn soon." The voice was craggy and raspy, robotic with just enough life to it to make tears run down Marian's face. She took a deep breath and heaved the door wide open. The scream that echoed through the house was enough to shatter her own nerves.

For in puddles of blood in the middle of a bright white bed lay Rosalie. Her face was a contorted half-scream, her hair matted with copious amounts of blood. And in the middle of her chest was a pair of rusty, vintage-looking scissors. Marian backed away and whimpered.

"Your turn's coming," the whisper repeated, and Marian saw a flash of black hair, of a white nightgown, and of a girl with an eerie smile that seemed to assure her she just might be. The figure giggled wildly once more before leaving, and Marian sank to the floor. She thought for a long moment about burning down the house with herself inside, just to make it stop.

Just make it stop, she sobbed internally, rocking herself and wondering what the next step would be.

Chapter Thirteen
Anne

Tears fell as Anne stared out the window, the porch light illuminating the blowing snow. It was all her fault. She felt it in her aching bones that the girl's death, the one Marian had found, was all her fault. She'd started this years ago when she'd done what she'd done to Rachel. The girl *was* a bad seed. There was no denying it. But was Anne any better? Especially after what she did in the end?

She rocked on the edge of her bed, staring out into the blackness. Her daughter and granddaughter were in the kitchen now, the police having just left them after hours of questioning. They were searching for a killer, the town on red alert after that girl's murder. But Anne knew. Her mind might not focus sometimes, might not be able to recall the important things. She couldn't remember what her heart condition was called or how many pills to take. She didn't know their address or their phone number, and try as she might, she couldn't remember what they'd eaten for breakfast. Still, her mind was clear on this one point.

There was no physical killer to be arrested. Rachel had done it.

Why had Candace insisted on getting that ornament down, and why hadn't anyone stopped her? That evil bell that had been banished to the attic along with the memory of the black-haired twin, the betrayal, and the dark Christmas she didn't like to think about. She should've known that it would bring trouble, a harbinger of death and destruction just like Rachel herself had been. She could hear Candace crying in the kitchen. Tears wouldn't fix this, though. Anne knew what would fix this. It was time to set things straight, to quiet the demons of the past.

Anne's legs quavered as she slowly stood from her bed, walking toward the window to look out one more time. Her fingers touched the chilled glass, sending a shiver through her. The snow was falling in a mesmerizing blast of white, and she could hear the Elvis song, her favorite, playing in her mind. This is how she would leave them—a snow falling, a serene quietude that could only be found with the final usurping of the demon she'd unleashed. How would it work? Would she join Rachel? Or was this Rachel's punishment for a dark life she couldn't leave behind?

Anne drew a streak on the foggy window, feeling the smoothness of the glass. She didn't know what the pills were called, but they were potent. Marian kept them in her room, away from Anne so she didn't accidentally take too many. But that was before the chaos distracted her daughter. That was before she had bigger problems to think about, such as police questions and a dead girl and a sobbing Candace. Anne hated the distress her daughter was in, would be in after she was gone.

But if things were ever going to be set right, this had to be done. It was the only way.

Anne walked to the dresser and pulled open the drawer. She shoved aside the random collection of items she'd hoarded over the past month. Scissors and tape from wrapping gifts, old letters she'd stowed away. A birthday card she'd bought at the dollar store for Marian's birthday next month. She rooted through to the very back, pulling out the orange bottle she'd stashed behind all the clutter. She didn't know how many pills to take, but she was certain it wasn't half a bottle. She hoped it wouldn't be too painful, that she would slip off to sleep and, with her parting, her twin's spirit would finally be gone. Marian and Candace would move on from the horrific events. They would rebuild a new Christmas tradition, one with happiness, just as Anne had all those years ago. Time wouldn't heal, but it would patch over the pain enough. It would have to be enough.

She sauntered to the bed, thinking about her life. Hoping Charlie would be there to greet her when she closed her eyes. So many years he'd been gone. She barely remembered his face. She twisted the bottle, struggling with the child lock. Darn it, her worn fingers couldn't grasp it. Tears of frustration welled. It was depressing to be so useless, so weak. She couldn't even kill herself properly without help.

As she was struggling with the bottle, there was a thudding on the window. She ignored the tree branch, biting her lip as she pulled and twisted, twisted and pulled. The pounding grew more insistent. It had been blustery, but not that windy. She looked up for a moment, and then the pills fell from her hand.

The black hair thudded and thudded against the window, and then it stopped. The girl looked up, and even through the frosty window, Anne could see the blood in her eyes, the smile on her face that was unnaturally wide. Her heart raced in her chest as Rachel's fingernails etched the glass, leaving streaks of blood and slime.

"What do you want?" Anne asked, shaking her head as she found the courage to walk toward the window. It didn't matter now. She had nothing to lose. Her life didn't matter. "Kill me, if that's what you want. You wretched girl, just kill me and be done with it."

Anne beat on the window now, emboldened. But there was nothing there. Rachel had vanished, leaving behind a single streak of blood that was caked in snow. The mix of evil and beauty was overpowering, and Anne cried out. She leaned on the sill, squeezing her eyes shut. How had this happened? After all these years, what did Rachel want with them? Why was she after innocent people? This wasn't about Marian or Candace or those girls. It was between them. It was about a sister's love gone wrong, a sister's need for revenge.

"Take me," she said breathlessly into the empty room.

And then the hairs on her neck stood up, her skin prickling.

"I will, Sister dearest," a haggard voice whispered in her ear so close, she could feel the breath.

She whirled on her foot and was face to face with Rachel, her porcelain face decayed in spots. Her eyes glowed, blood dripping from the corners. She looked like the twin sister that haunted Anne's memories, but she also didn't. She was a cross between the fog of memories and an elusive present.

"Take me," Anne begged, the figure in white made all the more ghoulish by her stiff, unrelenting grin.

"I will. But there's more you have to pay, first. You owe me. You need to suffer first. You'll all suffer."

"Rachel, please. It was so long ago. I'm sorry."

"You will be, you bitch. Just you wait. I'll take them all, one by pretty one."

Anne shook her head, at the mercy of a wicked spirit that once belonged to a malevolent girl.

"Mother was right," Anne heaved through clenched teeth. "We should have made you disappear even sooner."

And with that, Anne was against the window, her skull cracking against the glass as Rachel overpowered her, holding her throat until Anne could scarcely breathe. Rachel's right hand held the rusty scissors Anne had seen in her nightmares when she thought of Rachel. Were they the ones—? She didn't have time to consider it. The point of the scissors poked toward her eye, Rachel's cold breath chilling her neck.

"You bitch, can't you see? It was you who was the wicked one. You were one too many. If you'd have disappeared, it would have been different. It wasn't me, Anne. It was you. You know what you did. And now, you'll pay. You'll see."

Tears fell as Anne's ragged body shook violently, as the rusty point inched closer and closer toward her eye. She winced at the thought of the sharp point stabbing into her delicate, squishy eyeball.

"Mother?" a voice called from the hallway. Anne gasped and fought for breath, trying to free a scream. Trying to warn her daughter.

Rachel grinned. "The time will come, and you won't be able to stop it. And they'll all believe me. They'll know that this time, it *was* me."

All at once, her throat was free, and the scissors were gone. There was no trace of Rachel. If she didn't know better, she'd have thought she lost her mind. But she was there. Her trembling hands, the smell of death lingering in the room. Anne knew it had been real. She screamed and screamed. She didn't stop until her throat was ragged, until Marian and Candace were sobbing at her side, trying to get her into bed.

They thought she'd lost her mind. Maybe she had. Maybe they all had.

The truth, though, was so much worse.

They were all going to die. But first, they would suffer at the hands of a vile girl who wanted nothing more than revenge, who thirsted for evil.

A girl whom Anne had betrayed in the worst way imaginable.

Chapter Fourteen
Anne
1955

A nne sat with her sister on the picnic blanket, watching the sun set. The mastiff named Henry whom they'd just pet frolicked in the distance with his owner, catching a frisbee. Anne smiled at the sight. The fading rays shimmered in the background, shining from the glossy black hair that Rachel wore loose today. Her sister nibbled the crust of a peanut butter sandwich, staring at the lake. She was quiet, solemn, peaceful. Anne took a deep breath. It was good to see her like that. If only it could always be this simple, this quiet.

Dad had a rare day off from work and decided a trip to the lake would do perfectly. Rachel had beamed when he'd told her to get the basket ready, but Mother had glowered from the corner. Usually, when Dad wasn't around, Rachel wasn't a part of family outings. She'd done enough to embarrass the family, Mother always pointed out. Rachel was still doing penance for deeds unpunished, at least in Mother's eyes.

Now, the girls sat on the blanket, twin sisters without a connection. Some twins Anne knew seemed to be able to read each other's minds, to know exactly what they were thinking. The twin connection, though, had skipped them because sitting by Rachel, Anne realized she barely recognized her as a sister let alone as her twin. Such a shame, she thought sometimes, that the potential for a connection like that was lost. But Rachel was different, aloof, by choice, Anne reminded herself. It was her fault things weren't great between them.

Mother and Dad were off to the side near a tree, arguing as was their custom. Mother blamed that on Rachel, too, claiming Rachel acted differently than normal when Dad was around.

"Nice day," Anne whispered, ignoring the argument and trying to make conversation.

Rachel turned to look at her. "She's going to kill me some day, you know that don't you?"

And there it was. The darkness crushing the light. Why couldn't she just enjoy the day? Why couldn't Rachel just ever let them enjoy the day?

"Don't be insane, Rachel. What are you talking about?"

"Mother. She's always wanted to kill me, but she's afraid Dad won't forgive her. Someday, though, she's going to find a way."

"Rachel, stop. Stop playing the victim. You bring this on yourself. Why can't you ever be normal? Did you ever consider that?" Anne shook her head, setting down her soggy egg salad sandwich and pinching the bridge of her ramrod straight nose. Wasn't she ever tired of the turmoil, of the drama? Why couldn't she just be normal? It was the question they'd spent their lives asking.

"You think this is my fault? Of course you do. That's what happens when you're the chosen one. Do you ever think what it's like to be me? Always out the outs. Always the unwanted one. The one too many, the one no one wanted or wants now?"

Anne turned to look at Rachel, seeing her vulnerability and pain up close. Her heart panged a little bit at her words. She wanted to reach out for Rachel, to tell her it would be okay. She wanted to offer to leave with her and start fresh somewhere, two sisters like they were always meant to be. Anne thought maybe she was right. Maybe her sister wasn't the problem. For once in her life with the distance and a new vantage point, Anne looked at their mother, wondering how she'd missed it all along. But before she could turn and make things better, the cutting words interrupted.

"Let's go, girls. We're going home. Now." Mother ended the picnic early, Dad sulking behind. Rachel and Anne obediently packed up, knowing it was no use arguing at this point. When Mother set her mind to something, they all obeyed. That's just how it was. Better to get in the car and go home than be witness to the boiling scene that was brewing.

The ride home was silent, the four of them stewing in separate but connected worlds. Rachel plucked at a thread on her worn skirt, and Anne leaned her head back, staring up and wondering how she'd lived her life so long and hadn't seen what a dysfunctional mess it all was.

She was tired of thinking of whose fault it was. It needed to end. They weren't happy, never would be. Something had to change.

Anne didn't know that one week later, that change would come—it just wouldn't be the change to set things right like she'd hoped.

Chapter Fifteen
Candace

The funeral wouldn't be until after the holidays because the police were still investigating. The town was in an uproar over the murder of Rosalie, and Marian had been questioned ad nauseum about the discovery. Candace lay in bed, sickened with grief and angered that they'd been entwined in it.

What the police didn't know was that they'd never find the killer unless they looked to the supernatural realm. But Candance, Marian, Anne, and Eva knew the truth. Most of all, they knew that most likely, they were next on the list of victims. They were all about to become cold cases that would never be solved.

Candace had heard ghost stories growing up. She'd watched *The Blair Witch Project* with her friends, screaming nonsensically and giggling. But ghosts weren't real, and they certainly didn't kill people. Even now, it seemed ludicrous to believe. Believe it they did, though. Because Rachel had made her presence known. She was out for revenge.

But for what?

They'd tried prying the information out of Grandma Anne, but her lucidity was fading. Perhaps from the stress of the situation, or perhaps from the other unseen monster that was taking her away, piece by piece—her dementia. Still, they didn't know any more than they had when Candace had naively unboxed that hellish Christmas bell.

It really didn't matter, though, that they were in the dark about Rachel's motives, Candace thought as she pulled herself out of bed to wander to the kitchen for more coffee. Even if they knew Rachel's agenda, how would they stop her? How could they calm a being whom they didn't even begin to understand?

Candace's mother sat at the table, weary and pale. No one had slept at all, between the police investigation, the horrors of the death, and the fear that Rachel would come for them.

There'd been a few rustlings last night—footsteps, whispers, and blinking lights on the tree. But overall, it had been quiet, calm. Candace dared to hope that maybe Rachel was done—she'd slaughtered her victim. Maybe this was the end. Deep down, though, the words Marian had heard echoed.

They were next. It wasn't over. Perhaps it was even worse that Rachel hadn't come last night, that the house had been silent and peaceful. The anticipation was always worse than the actual deed, after all.

A soft rapping on the door interrupted Candace's stilted words she was about to spew at her mother.

"I'll get it," Candace replied, weary and terrified to open the door and see what new horrors awaited them.

When the door creaked open, her eyes landed on Eva, but it took her a moment to process it all. Usually tidy and streamlined in appearance, Eva wore pajama pants, a bath robe, and bags under her eyes. Her hair was in a frizzy bun, and she looked even paler than yesterday. It made sense. Rosalie and Eva had, of course, stayed close friends even after Candace was long gone. Candace automatically wrapped her friend in a hug, leading the weeping woman into the kitchen as Marian stood to greet her.

"I'm sorry," Eva apologized. "I just didn't know where to go."

"Sit, sit," Marian ordered, life coming back to her face at the prospect of having something to focus on. The three sat in the weathered kitchen chairs, teary silence resonating louder than a conversation. Finally, Eva broke the quiet.

Tears crashing on the wooden table as she blankly stared at the center of it, she murmured three words. "It was her."

"What?" Candace asked, worried about Eva's mental state now.

"It was the black-haired girl. She killed Rosalie."

Marian studied Candace. They hadn't talked to Eva since the discovery yesterday, hadn't told anyone what Marian suspected. But Eva stated it as fact, not as a question.

"How do you know?" Candace asked hesitantly, reaching over to touch her friend's hand.

"Because she was in my house last night. I saw her when I went to the bathroom. The black-haired girl, the one I started seeing after the ornament."

"Rachel," Candace whispered. Eva looked up with a start.

"We think it's my Grandma's twin sister," she offered, and Eva nodded, as if that made complete sense. All of their rational lines of thinking had been deadened. They were willing to accept just about anything as the truth.

Eva played with the ring on her finger, twisting it as she stared blankly ahead, only pausing to swipe at a tear once or twice. "She told me she did it. That she killed Rosalie."

Marian nodded. "I saw her too. When I found Rosalie."

Eva looked up, eyeing Marian with an oxymoronic combination of pain and happiness—pain at the mention of her deceased friend, but happiness that she wasn't alone. Misery always loves company, and most humans just want validation for what they see and feel. Eva was no different.

"She told me that she killed her. I just—I don't understand. Why?"

"We don't know either. That's what we're trying to figure out."

Eva stood from the table now, wandering to the kitchen window to look out into the day. The snow still covered the ground, a thin, bright layer. Today, though, the sun was shining down, beaming off the snow in a blinding phenomenon.

"There's more," she said. "She told me I'm next." Eva turned at the words, her body shaking. Marian exhaled loudly, turning to Candace. Candace's heart pounded as she stood, too, to cross the room and wrap Eva in her arms.

"What do we do?" Eva asked, sobbing. "How do we stop this? I told Pat what I'm dealing with, and he thinks I've lost my mind. He said it's just stress, but I heard him on the phone with my mother. He wants to have me committed. I just . . . what am I supposed to do?"

"I don't know," Candace whispered, her voice cracking as she held her friend in her arms. What were any of them going to do? It seemed hopeless.

"We need to figure this out. We need to get to the bottom of this," Marian answered for them. Candace felt like her mother was a broken record, repeating an impossible task like that would make it more possible.

Eva, why don't you stay with us? It might be safer here, where we can figure it all out. Rachel doesn't want you. She wants to get back at Grandma Anne. We just need to sort out why. Call Pat, tell him you're staying with a friend, not to worry," Marian ordered.

"Okay," Eva replied. Candace saw the concern on her face, but it lifted a little bit at being told what to do. Marian could make anyone feel like she was in control. Staying with them was Eva's only really option, but it wasn't perfect. And Candace secretly feared that her friend staying with them was the beginning of the end for them all.

"I'll get Grandma Anne. She needs to tell us the truth if we're going to sort through this."

Candace and Eva sat back down. Tonight was Christmas Eve, but no one felt like celebrating or talking. Candace looked past Eva at the tree, thinking about how it had all started with a beat-up box in the attic. She should have never come home. Maybe if she hadn't, Rosalie would still be alive. Eva would be with her fiancé, getting ready for a cozy holiday at home, and her mother would be just fine.

She'd put them all in danger coming home, and she didn't have any idea how to fix it.

She'd brought hell to the holidays instead of joy, and now, the truth settled into Candace's heart.

They were all going to die. It was just a matter of how and when.

Chapter Sixteen
Marian

They sat in the living room, gathered around Grandma Anne's chair as if it were story time. This story time, though, was demented and more important than ever. They needed answers, and they needed them now. A girl had died. Marian wouldn't let another person die for the demented, confusing cause. She didn't quite know what she could do about the situation, even with all of the information, but she had to try. Damn it, she had to try.

"Mother, please. We need to know. Maybe if we understand Rachel, we can figure out what she wants."

Anne looked up at her daughter, peering at her in a way that made Marian quake.

"She wants me to suffer. She wants us all to die," Anne said, and then the rocking began again. In an hour, they hadn't gotten any further, Anne too upset to talk. Marian was getting frustrated.

"We need to know. It might be hard, but you need to tell us the truth. Tell us what happened."

"Wicked girl, wicked girl," Anne started chanting, staring at the ornament on the tree. She rocked back and forth, back and forth, faster and faster until the chair threatened to upend. Tears mixed with the frothing spit coming from her mouth. She looked rabid and sounded hoarse. Her voice shrill and unearthly, the words kept flying out of her mouth on repeat as if she were stuck in a trance. Marian had enough. She didn't have time for this.

Stomping to the tree, she plucked the ornament off that her mother was staring at. She told herself it didn't matter, that they were already screwed, but when her skin made contact with the ornament, the jolt that went through her reminded her of why it was a terrible idea.

Her stomach roiled and her head felt as if it would explode, the images flashing through her mind at lightning speed. She heard screams this time, and at first, she thought they were her own. But these were screams of a younger girl, pleading for her life. The blood, the scissors, the black, stringy hair. Over and over they whirled about, but she couldn't drop the ornament. It was burning into her skin, seared into her as if it was hot glued there. Her hands shook violently, and she heard Candace calling her in the background. But before she could drop it or fling it or throw it through the window, she felt herself tumbling to the ground, felt the thud of her head on the living room floor, felt the searing pain all through her body. And a few moments later, when the ornament had been flung from her hands by Candace and the room had stopped spinning, she sat up, clarity in her mind.

Candace shook her arm.

"Mom, talk to me. Are you okay?"

She ignored the fear in her daughter's voice, ignored the shouts of Eva and the tears. She brushed aside the pain in her head and her heart as she looked at her mother, seeing her with new, darkened perspective. Because when she'd toppled to the floor, in the middle of the montage of horrifying images, she'd seen Rachel. She'd heard Rachel's ragged voice whispering a harsh truth that shocked Marian to the core. Suddenly, so much made sense, even though it made sense in the most demented, terrifying of ways.

She shakily got to her feet against Candace's wishes. She paraded across the plush tan carpet, her bare feet cascading across it as she beelined for the chair. She leaned down with both hands on the arms of the chair and inched her face closer and closer to her mother. Where she'd always seen kind eyes full of love and truth, she saw something else now. A darkness that filled her with rage. This was all Anne's fault. They were all going to pay the ultimate price because of the secret Anne had hidden her entire life. As she came face to face with the woman who had raised her, the woman she apparently didn't know at all, anger bubbled in her throat.

Marian whispered the words that changed everything. And finally, after the words had escaped, it was like Anne was transported back to full mental clarity. After the harsh accusation had escaped her lips, Marian returned to her seat across from her mother. Candace and Eva stared, frozen in place. One couldn't hear a thing except for the hum of the furnace and everyone's breathing. The icy silence walled up between them, the four women peered at each other with stoicism. And it was only after a long moment that Anne audibly exhaled and began telling the entire story, the truth that no one wanted to hear but needed to in order to clean up the mess Anne had made of all of their lives.

Chapter Seventeen
Anne
1955

Things had calmed into the typical routine in the house. Dad was back working his long hours at the firm, and Mother was her typical self with Rachel. Anne had settled on the sofa with a book, the rain interminable on that July day. Rachel was in their room, tucked out of reach of Mother's angry curses.

The phone rang, and Mother skipped to it, no doubt anxious to catch up on the neighborhood gossip with that awful woman, Sandy, she insisted on chatting with. Anne flipped the page in her book, hoping that Derek would come and rescue her later for a trip to the Milkshake Hut. Anything to get away from the oppressive tone in the house.

"What?!" Mother exclaimed in the phone, her face paling. Anne looked up, wondering if someone had died. Rachel even came running from their room, leaning on the doorframe in the kitchen and studying their mother. She looked to her sister, but Anne shrugged.

"I see. Well, you know that's not true. But I'll have a word with her." Mother's face turned grim, and the anger seethed in her eyes. She glowered at Rachel, a hatred bubbling so strong, it was palpable in the air. Rachel took a step backward as Mother slammed the phone down.

"So, Rachel. That was Sandy. Turns out we're the talk of the town. Would you happen to know why?" Her inhalations were deep, her words uttered without even a pretense of calm. Anne closed the book and set it aside, the movement subtle and soft so as to not draw attention. Her stomach dropped as she grabbed the hem of her dress tightly, playing with the fabric to keep herself grounded. She could sense that this was different, that they were on the edge of something momentous.

Rachel stood apathetic, defiant, as if a sense of strength had finally emerged within her. Anne noted that her shoulders were straighter, her chin up as if she were ready to march out into the world and claim it. She glowered right back at her mother wordlessly, tapping her toe as if challenging her to the battle that was about to ensue.

"She says that you were at the Milkshake Hut yesterday with someone. Care to indulge?"

Rachel shrugged. "Yeah. Stephanie and I were there."

"Oh really?"

Rachel took a step forward. "Yes. We were. And you know why, Mother? Because I love her."

Anne shuddered in shock. It was true, Rachel rejected any boy in a ten-foot radius, but Anne didn't know what to think. A girl? Really? Was it true? Or was she just trying to rattle Mother? Because in Mother's perfect, white-picket fence world where her

two daughters grew up to be the perfect housewives and mothers,
Anne knew this would certainly disturb things.

Mother ignored her, stepping forward. The two were inches
away from each other in the kitchen, both standing their ground.
Anne stayed put, watching it all unravel like never before.

"And you were kissing her? Is that true?"

"Yes, Mother. I was. So what?"

"So what?" their mother asked, giggling frenetically, as if
deranged. "So what? Do you know what this means for our
family? Do you know what people will say?"

"Is that all you care about? What people think? Don't you
care about my happiness at all, not even a little?"

"I care about what you've done to this family. I care that
you've done everything you can to ruin us. And now this. What
will your father think? Have you thought of that?"

Rachel took another step forward, forcing her Mother
backward against the counter in a hard and fast dance neither
knew the steps to.

"You know what he'll think? He'll think good. At least
someone in this family has fucking love, real love. Do you think
he loves you? Do you think he doesn't see what a selfish, horrible
woman you are? He doesn't love you. Wake up. He never has. He
only stays to keep up appearances, to keep the office from talking
about his affair with Catherine."

A silence took over in the room, all cards on the table. Anne
watched the tension and hatred from the past seventeen years
rupture. The truth about it all had come out, and there was no
going back. For a moment, Mother stood, cold and shriveled, hit
at the core. Rachel had said what everyone had tried to ignore for
so many years. The picture-perfect family was unraveling before

Anne's very eyes, and her stomach sank at the prospect of what was to come.

However, true to her stubborn will, her mother then rose up, standing tall. Her body quavered as she stared with pure hatred in her eyes, her stance matching Rachel's defiant pose. They were two lionesses squaring off in a fight for the pride, and Anne was simply a helpless spectator.

"If our relationship has faltered, it's only because of you. You're the problem here. Don't you see? You've ruined all of our lives. You've ruined them all." Her mother's words were cold but quiet, as if she were declaring a statement of fact instead of a cutting phrase.

There was no warning, no pause. There was no verbal retaliation as one would expect. Before Anne could scream or even understand what was happening, the kitchen knife was in her mother's hands, Rachel pinned against the counter. The knife was poised above Rachel, and for a moment, Anne thought about what a weird picture it would make. A mother, a daughter, and a knife. How had it come to this? Rachel fought back, clawed at her mother as if her life depended on it. It did. Because their mother had a rage, an undying thirst for Rachel's blood. That much was apparent now. Anne ran between them.

"Stop," she screamed, thrusting herself in the middle, half expecting the knife to bite into her flesh. The word was enough. Her mother stopped, and a silence re-entered the room. As if they were in a still frame, they stood, Anne in the middle as she had always been. After a few breaths, the three women's tears started to slip out, Rachel and Mother panting on either side of her. The knife was tossed on the counter with a metallic clang, a relic of what almost was and what could never be again. The knife may as

well have sliced all three of their throats, Anne thought. Because the family was as good as dead. They were all as good as dead now.

Anne expected Rachel to rampage, to scream, to threaten. She worried about retaliation, about a psychotic break. But things were even worse. Rachel, tears falling, slunk backward, the poignant pose dismantled. She shook visibly as she edged toward their bedroom. Sadness melted her face, and Anne's heart broke.

She stared at her mother, waiting for what would happen next. Hoping her mother could fix this like she used to fix Anne's messy hair or scratched knee.

"I'm sorry. I just—this can't go on. Your sister has problems." The words were distant and insolent in a way Anne couldn't understand. Anne stared at her, wondering how it must feel to be her. To have such an anger toward your own child. A mother's love is supposed to be unconditional. But what if it wasn't in some cases? Whose fault was it, the mother or the child? Anne's head and heart were heavy. She nodded at her mother, a stranger in so many ways now, and walked away. She threw open the screen door and headed to the porch in the downpour, letting the water pound down onto her skin.

IT WAS A LONG AFTERNOON waiting for Dad to get home. Anne was terrified of what would happen. Would their mother go to jail? Would Dad send her away? Would they all fall into a heap of tears, realizing things needed to change, that Rachel needed help, but so did all of them? The car pulled up, and Dad came skipping into the house. Anne didn't say a word, soaked to the bone. Usually, Mother would scold her for being out in the wet,

threatening that hypothermia and death came from being that cold. Her mother, though, had been absent all afternoon, tucked away in some corner of the house as had Rachel. They'd all spent their time alone, processing what had happened. But Dad's return would forcibly break that silence, and Anne needed to bear witness to what would become of the family, good or bad. Swiping at a piece of hair stuck to her forehead, she stood, turned on her heel, and followed her father as he unknowingly headed into the heat of the battle.

Mother was perched on the couch with a cup of coffee and a tear-stained face. Rachel was apparently still in the bedroom.

"What's going on?" Dad asked, and the two women in the area just stared silently. Anne awaited her mother's confession. She waited for Dad's anger, then hurt, then his solution. They needed a solution.

Mother looked up, tears still flowing. "Rachel tried to kill me."

Anne froze, looking at the woman who was now even more unrecognizable than the woman she'd seen with the knife this afternoon. She shook her head, wanting to open her mouth.

"What?" Dad asked, incredulous, putting down his briefcase. "What the hell are you talking about?"

Anne sat, feeling as though she were having an out-of-body experience as their mother told the story. The knife. The threats. The almost stabbing. But in her version of events, Rachel was the monster, and she the victim. Rachel had grabbed the knife, had tried to slit Mother's throat until Anne had stepped in. When the story was done, Dad called for Rachel. Anne felt vomit bubbling in her throat. She felt the truth clawing its way up her throat, pinching with each step up. But her lips were glued shut. She couldn't speak, couldn't find a way to spit out the words. She sat, an unwilling observer.

"Is this true?" he asked, looking at Rachel after summarizing the events Mother had uttered.

Tears fell from Rachel's eyes. "It's not true, Dad. It's not. She tried to kill me!"

Dad stood in the middle of the three women, clearly taken back by the turn of events, how a random July day could change everything.

"Ask Anne. She was here," Rachel said, sobbing.

Anne turned to her sister, seeing the pity and the pain on her face. She opened her mouth to speak. She looked to her mother, also filled with pity and pain. Her mother's eyes, puffy and red from tears, pleaded with her wordlessly.

Something needs to change.

One too many.

She's out of control.

Thoughts of the past seventeen years swirled in Anne's head. Rachel and her mother were both a mess, Anne now understood. She looked at the woman perched on the couch who had a knife to her own daughter's throat not too long ago. And true. Rachel had done some messed up things in her life, but so had their mother. What was the right answer?

Anne looked at Rachel and saw all of the frightening outbursts, all of the psychotic breaks. She thought of all the times she hadn't been able to sleep knowing her sister was in the same room, knowing what her sister was capable of. Was Mother really to be faulted for snapping today, for growing tired of it all? Mother was just looking out for all of them, for their reputations, something Rachel didn't understand the importance of. If Rachel stayed, what could it mean for Anne? Derek would never be permitted to marry a girl from a family with a ruined reputation. Maybe it was time she looked out for herself.

"Rachel did it, Dad. She tried to kill Mother." The words were out before she could second-guess her decision. The fates sealed. Dad crumpled to the floor, and Rachel let out a war cry.

"You know it's not true. You damned fools. You'll regret this. I would expect this from her," Rachel pointed to their mother, "but not you, Anne. I'm your twin. I'm your sister. How could you?"

Anne's heart cracked, and she ran outside, needing the rain to wash away the pain, the guilt, everything. If only she'd been born to a different family where she wasn't forced to make this choice. She sank to the ground, the water puddling around her, chilling her to the core as she listened to the wails of her sister.

Chapter Eighteen
Marian

"So I did kill her," Anne wailed now as the story finished. "I killed her because my lie sent her back to that awful place, The Redwood Asylum. That's where she died a few months later. It was my fault. I told the lie that sealed her fate."

Marian's heart sank as she saw the pain on her mother's face. It was a complicated tale, but not what Marian had expected when she'd chanted those words from the vision of Rachel: "You killed her." She was simultaneously relieved and terrified that her mother hadn't killed Rachel in the sense of the word she'd expected.

It was obvious why Rachel wasn't at peace, why she wanted revenge. But the fuzzier, murkier part of the equation was: How did they set things right? How did they avenge Rachel, make her feel at peace? And could they? Marian rubbed the bridge of her nose, closing her eyes to think. She needed to save the family. But what did one do in this situation? An exorcism? Tonight was Christmas Eve. She didn't think there would be time.

She glanced to the tree in the corner, still shuddering at the ornament, now resting underneath its branches. It all started with the Christmas bell. They'd been in peace for so many decades until Candace brought it down. She still thought that was the answer. Burning it hadn't done it, and destroying it was out of the question. But what if they made an offering?

"I have an idea," she whispered into the room of battered, broken, and terrified women.

And then she told them the plan—a weak plan, true, but the only one they had.

Chapter Nineteen
Anne

Pressing her face against the cold glass, Anne stared out into the dark abyss. They would have to park at the edge of the grounds for it wouldn't do to be caught trespassing, not here. She studied the iron gate, peeling but still broadcasting its strength. It looked like it was made to keep in rather than keep out, a foreboding thought that made Anne cringe.

What had she felt all those years ago, when Dad drove her up this very same road toward her impending doom? Had she thought of Anne, thought of revenge? A sadness usurped Anne's thoughts, and suddenly she knew. Despondency. That was at the root of who Rachel was.

She'd heard the stories over the years of this archaic piece of the town, the stone building hidden on the outskirts of Oakwood that everyone tried to forget about. Back when Rachel was sent there, it truly was a place you were sent to be forgotten. Troubled girls, criminally insane, and dangerous people were dropped by their family members, most of which were of the elite class and could afford such an expensive but discreet institution. They would cast out their unwanted family members and then drive out of the dark forest and back to their sunshine yellow lives. The town had their legends, their ghost stories about this haunted ground. Anne had always tried to ignore the stories, preferring, like her family, to tuck Rachel and Redwood Asylum safely in the past, where it belonged. Thus, Anne had gone on and lived her life, forgetting about the patch of ground and the people who were locked in behind the iron gate.

With the grounds of Redwood staring at her, it was all coming back full circle. For at the end of Anne's life, Rachel was trying to destroy it. She was trying to make Anne feel the pain and anger and terror she must have felt.

Marian parked the car at the edge of the iron fence around the side of the property. The forest was so thick, you couldn't even see the foreboding building, but Anne had heard enough about it to have a clear image in her mind. The stone walls were a fortress for the disturbed. Now, she hoped this place would be a final reconciliation, a Christmas olive branch to the dead sister who was out for blood.

Chapter Twenty
Candace

"Are you sure this is going to work?" Candace asked her mother, knowing the answer but not wanting to hear it.

"It has to," her mother whispered in a solemn voice. She carried the original box that had started it all. It was an ordinary, brown box, the kind one would receive books and perfume and every other household item in. But now, it housed the rusty remnants of an ornament that should've stayed in the attic forever.

They'd scooped it into the box after her mother unleashed her plan. Even without touching it, Candace felt a jolt of its power, of its demented malice, as she'd used a magazine to transfer it to the box. They'd taped it shut and prayed to a merciless God that they'd never see it again.

Grandma Anne had insisted on making the trek to the edge of town on a mission more dangerous than any would admit. It made sense, though, which was why her mother had agreed. In many ways, this was Grandma Anne's battle. She needed to be there to make the offering and right the wrong. Because if she didn't, they would all pay.

Candace felt more peaceful about her possible demise at this point. There was a sense of acceptance that came with the knowledge that things would be what they were, that she wasn't in control. Her mother had begged her to leave and go back to New York, which told her just how dire the situation was. After all of Marian's begging to spend the holidays together, her willingness to sacrifice the holiday helped Candace know the truth—the plan wouldn't work. They were all doomed, and there was no one to save them.

Her father had been a monster they could escape from, in the end. Despite his violent nature and what he almost did, he wasn't successful. They were able to outrun him, outsmart him, and, eventually, the scars of their fear faded. This was different. This was an enemy unseen with an unquenchable thirst for revenge that passed over into the next life. Who were they to think they could beat that force?

Still, standing at the edge of The Redwood Psychiatric Hospital, as the name had been changed twenty years ago, Candace inhaled the frosty air as her mother stood with the box. There was a coldness here, looking into the thick forest, but it wasn't just the time of year. It was as if Redwood existed on the edge of Earth, a forgotten ledge in society that everyone was blinded to. How many souls were forgotten here? How many troubled minds wouldn't sleep peacefully tonight? How much had her great aunt suffered at the hands of an injustice, of a mother who didn't love her, and of a family who let her down?

Certainly, there was a wickedness to Rachel. But underneath her terror and anger for what Rachel had done to Rosalie, for what she would probably do to them all, there rested something else. Maybe it was the holiday season still clinging to life in her heart, but Candace felt a wash of sorrow for the girl who troubled them now. She hoped this would bring her peace.

Eva had decided not to come, claiming it was probably best if only family went along. Perhaps it was the truth, or maybe the girl was just too terrified by the prospect of stepping so close to the place her own sister had once worked at. Eva had heard the stories, which she'd passed to Candace. The residents of Redwood had become legends in their own right. It was only standing on the actual ground that one remembered they weren't just fictionalized characters—they were people in a real-life archaic haunt of the modern day.

So they'd dropped Eva at her house, where she would gather some clothes since Pat was at work. She would return to them, just to make sure the plan worked and that Rachel didn't resurface. She wanted to stay away from Pat, partially because he was concerned about her mental health, but also because she wanted to protect him. Candace could appreciate that selfless level of love, her mind going to Landon. What would he think of all of this? In some ways, she wished he was here to make her feel safe.

Anne stood in the middle of them now as they faced Redwood, the wind picking up as they shoved hands in their pockets. Marian took a solemn step forward, setting the box just outside the fence. It was the best they could do.

"Rachel, we offer this gift as a sign of our sorrow and forgiveness. Please rest in peace."

The words seemed to fall short, apparently even to Marian's ears, because she shrugged her shoulders and turned to Candace. No one knew how to handle the situation.

Candace took a deep breath, waiting. She didn't know what she expected. The wild whisper in the wind? The angry apparition to appear and float away? In truth, she just wanted a sign to validate their belief this would solve it all. The proof did not come.

Grandma Anne finally broke the silence.

"I'm sorry, Rachel. I am. I made a mistake. Please don't hurt anyone else."

The words languidly made their way out of Grandma Anne's mouth, more like a prayer than a plea. They pierced Candace's heart as she thought about all the pain that had permeated time and space, all of the regrets and guilt and sorrows. Was this what every family was like, tarnished by the past and tormented in the present by a history of mistakes? It suddenly seemed like the familial bond was nothing more than a string of choices, good and bad, that haunted each generation. The wind stirred again, and the box sat, wettened by snow. It felt very anticlimactic when, after a long moment, Marian turned and walked to the car.

"Let's go home," she murmured, and the two women followed their leader, trusting their genuine actions would be enough.

Trusting that the holidays would be salvaged and, as painful as it was, they could leave the past at Redwood in a box by the side of the road.

Chapter Twenty-One
Marian

The drive felt interminable, all three women on edge. Marian turned up the radio to break the silence, but when a jolly song came on, she quickly snapped the knob off again. There wasn't a remnant of a holiday mood anywhere to be found in the car, after all. They all awaited what would happen next. Marian wasn't the religious type, but she said a silent prayer that this crazy scheme would work and that life would go back to normal.

She checked the rearview mirror repeatedly, both to keep an eye on Candace but also to see if there were any unwanted visitors. Every time her eyes fell on the reflective glass, she feared the worst and her stomach dropped like that time she'd ridden that insane rollercoaster with Candace at the park. But this ride was as calm and eventless as ever.

Pulling into the driveway and shutting off the car, the three sat looking at the house. It was the same, peeling siding and overgrown vegetation giving it a dark vibe. Still, it seemed even darker now, the thoughts of what it housed chilling her to the core. She reminded herself that it was all over and that the holidays would be uneventful. Mercifully uneventful.

The three women slowly got out of the car, and they walked by Eva's car. She'd returned, the poor thing. That was another situation to deal with, how she would handle Pat. What she would tell him. They'd have to sort through that. He must think she'd gone mad for sure, what with her up and leaving on Christmas Eve. But it couldn't be helped. They needed to protect her. They were in this together.

Walking through the front door, Marian's eyes scanned the terrain. She half expected to see Rachel standing in the middle of the kitchen, scissors in hand ready to finish them off. In some ways, it would be a blessing for it all to end. The waiting, the unknowing, was the worst.

"Eva?" Candace called into the silent house, and they all held their breath. No response except for a muffled, off-putting cry of agony from Muffin. It seemed to be coming from the living room.

Marian pushed forward as panic bubbled, the three women clustered like chickens on a rainy day. Perhaps they thought if they stuck together, all would be okay. Marian didn't take time to mull it over. They pushed to the living room, her eyes jumping to the tree. It was lit, but there was an empty branch where the thing had rested. She sighed in relief.

Until Candace gasped. Marian turned to see Candace shaking Eva's shoulder. The girl sat in Anne's chair, holding Muffin in her lap and stroking him. The first thing she noticed was the blood oozing all over Eva, who stared blankly ahead as if she'd passed on. Her eyes were glazed over, her face emotionless like she'd been carved in stone. Candace shook her, and Marian rushed to follow suit. Marian tried to figure out where Eva had been hurt, until Grandma Anne cried.

That's when she realized the blood was coming from Muffin. He'd been sliced and cut over and over. He was panting.

"Eva, honey, are you okay?" she asked, wanting to help Muffin but terrified for Eva, too. She felt the girl who was cold to the touch. She shook her arm, propped on the arm rest of the chair. There was no response, not a flutter or a twitch. Marian and Candace shook harder.

And then, Eva turned her head to the right, her glossy eyes peering into Marian's. But something wasn't quite right. The pupils were too big, way too big, the eyes appearing to be large black holes dotting Eva's porcelain skin.

"Welcome back, Marian. Did you really think you could get rid of me so fast?" Eva's lips spewed in the familiar, raspy voice that wasn't Eva's at all. Candace and Marian inched backward, processing the disconnect between Eva's body and the voice as she flung the dying cat against the living room wall. The three women shrieked at the sight of his black body flinging into the wall and then falling, the odd angles of his limbs and neck telling them all he had passed.

There was no time for mourning. The familiar, eerie giggle that was always off-tune echoed from her lips. It was sweet and soft at first, but as the women backed away from the body of Eva that clearly wasn't Eva at all, the giggle grew fiercer, nastier, deeper. It warped as Eva rocked violently, erratically. Her movements were so energetic that the chair seemed to leave the ground at times, and Marian was certain she would crash to the ground.

"Stupid fools, thinking you could leave the ornament as an offering. After what she did? You think that's what I want?" Eva's body jolted up from the chair, and the three women pressed against the living room wall.

"Stop it, stop it, stop it," Anne shouted, holding her ears and crying. Marian couldn't speak, fear overtaking her body as she reached for Candace's hand.

Eva ran so fast to them that she seemed to be floating. Just before she got to Candace, she stopped. An eerie, oversized grin painted itself on Eva's face and then, with a whip of the neck in an unnatural position, she stood, startled. Her eyes were back to normal. She gazed at the three of them.

"What happened?" Eva's voice returned, but Marian clutched Candace, holding her back. They couldn't trust this.

"It's okay," Marian whispered, looking at the girl. She tried to assess whether this was Eva, where Rachel had gone, what they should do.

"Wretched girl!" Anne shouted from the other side of Candace.

"Mom, it's okay. Why don't you sit down?" she said, carefully crossing over Candace to get to her mother. Anne needed to sit down, to calm down or this could all end terribly for her. She was too frail to handle this. But just as she was getting to Anne, a scream came out of the elderly woman's lips as she pointed to the ceiling.

Marian turned, as did Candace and Eva, to see the sight that Anne was gaping at.

Rachel crawled on the ceiling on all fours, her head turned at the wrong angle. Her bruised and battered face was drawn, but the familiar grin that stretched too far was present. She giggled, galloping on the ceiling, traversing it like a spider with its sight on its prey. Marian squeezed Anne's hand and nestled back, her eyes never leaving the black-haired demon.

Rachel at once leaped from the ceiling to the ground, standing behind Eva. Eva trembled, whimpering now as she stared into their eyes. Rachel's arm pulled her close, but Eva didn't struggle. She stood still, as if she could disappear.

"One too many. Always one too many," Rachel whispered as she coughed. Her cough was bone-racking, and after a long moment of spewing out blood, something solid landed in her hand.

Marian whimpered. The ornament, good as new, sitting in Rachel' slender fingers.

Rachel eyed it with delight, a giggle erupting as she rolled it between her bony, rigid fingers. She looked at Candace, at Anne, and finally at Marian. Marian squirmed under the monster's gaze, and then her mouth fell open as she screamed and shrieked, as they all did.

Because the ornament in Rachel's hands was suddenly shoved down Eva's throat, the girl's eyes bulging in shock and desperation as she struggled to fight back, to get away, to scream. They watched in terror as Rachel's arm stretched inexplicably and shoved the ornament down, the bulge in Eva's throat and her purpling face telling them what they already perhaps knew.

She was going to die.

Marian couldn't take it anymore. She leaped forward, grabbing Eva, trying to yank her away from the psychotic spirit. But it was no use. She yanked and pulled, but Rachel's power was too strong. With the bat of a hand, she flung Marian across the room like she was nothing but a crumb. Her ribs ached from slamming into the wall, but she got up again, screaming as Candace attempted the same maneuver.

Finally, after a long struggle for breath and a pleading look with her eyes, Eva's fight was done. She crumpled to the ground; the three women were horrified at being so close to their dead friend. The girl Marian was supposed to protect was gone, destroyed by the wretched being. Marian shook her head, glowering.

"You fucking monster," she screamed through tears, Candace a sobbing wreck on the floor next to her dead friend. "No wonder they locked you up."

Rachel snapped her neck to the right, grinning. Marian feared what was next, knowing it was probably her turn as promised. But Rachel simply continued to smirk, and then reached down for Eva. She forced her hand straight through Eva's neck, blood spewing as she rooted around in the dead body. She plucked the ornament from Eva's remains, dangling it for all to see.

Rachel flung the rusty ornament onto the tree, and it landed on its branch. It swayed back and forth, the lights flickering in a cacophony of bloody beauty. The night was bright, but it was not merry.

Rachel sauntered back wordlessly, staring at all three of them. They were too exhausted from terror to run, too shocked and traumatized to formulate a plan. Marian stared, wondering what good a plan would do anyway. There was no winning. They were all pawns in this twisted game, all chips in a game of roulette that was rigged.

Rachel smiled again, calmly and peacefully. The words were almost a promise as they escaped her bloody lips.

"Who's next?"

And Marian let the tears fall as she sank to the floor, wondering how everything could go so wrong.

Chapter Twenty-Two
Candace

Her hands were clutching her throat. Candace could feel the long, pointy nails clawing into her flesh, draining blood from her. *This is where I die,* she thought. *On top of my friend, on Christmas Eve, with my mother and grandma watching.*

Candace was a fighter, but this was too much. The nails slashed into her and a burning sensation travelled down the length of her throat as Rachel squeezed. She heard her mother and grandmother screaming, tearing at her as the beast lifted her by the throat, her legs kicking wildly. Even when one gives up, the will to survive is strongly instinctual. She scratched and gasped and tried to fight her way back to life.

Rachel dropped Candace's feet to the floor, her fingers still clasping her throat. She dragged her, and Candace opened her eyes to see her mother's horrified face as she was yanked back the hallway, past the familiar sights of home. Thrown in the guest room, Candace's cheek hit the carpet as the air left her lungs. Her head was spinning from the impact as Rachel slammed the door, her giggle echoing down the hall.

Candace gasped for air, her own hands rubbing her throat where the fingers had squeezed. She felt the hot, sticky blood and the burning of the wounds. She didn't think it was enough blood to kill her. At this point, what did it matter? Her cheek on the carpet of the guest room, she cried, listening to screams from her mother and grandmother, wondering what was happening. Angry that she couldn't stop it. Angry most of all at herself for her role in all of it.

She picked herself up and limped to the door. Her hands clutched at the knob.

Locked.

Solid.

She yanked and screamed pointlessly, but she needed to do something. She didn't care if she died trying. She kicked the door, shoving and pushing and pulling on the knob. It was no use. It wasn't opening.

To hell with it. She climbed under her bed, grasping the familiar baseball bat. Her fingers felt the smooth polish of the bat as she dashed across the room, knowing what she had to do. She crossed the room to the window, her mother's screams driving her forward. But just as she was about to bash out the window and jump to the icy tundra below, she was tossed once more to the floor. The wind knocked out of her in a sensation now familiar, she willed her body to scramble away, to get her to her feet again.

"Where do you think you're going?" a voice whispered, but when Candace turned, it wasn't the black-haired girl who was upon her. It was something else entirely.

Chapter Twenty-Three
Marian

Marian kicked the door once more, knowing it was futile. It was as if the door were welded shut, every budge and kick negligible against its strength. And with no window in the bathroom to be found, she was sealed in a tomb of despair. Still, her cell wasn't soundproof, and her stomach rolled again at the sound of Candace's shrieks of terror. Tears fell as Marian prayed for it to all end, for a miracle to happen, for this Christmas to be salvaged. She knew her wish was perhaps even vainer than her attempt to kick down the door.

She wiped her tears away, her heart and mind shriveling from the fact that she couldn't save Candace. She wanted to crawl out of her skin, to pull the very core of herself from its center and splay it open, a living sacrifice to end this maniacal chase. She would sacrifice it all if she could just quiet her daughter's screams as she'd done when Candace was young.

Marian had spent her life hovering and protecting, shielding her daughter from vile beings in the real world. Now, at the end of it all, it didn't matter. Evil would win in a sick, twisted turn of events. Rachel would win, and Anne's mothering instincts apparently were faulty after all.

But if Marian's mothering aptitude was faulty, what about Anne? She wanted to hate her mother for her role in this. If Anne had told her sooner, would that have changed things? If she'd have been a better sister, a better person, certainly they wouldn't be facing this darkness now. Still, Marian knew she wasn't one to judge. Her slate wasn't wiped clean, after all. She'd made her fair share of poor choices and, as some would argue, even some sinister ones.

She leaned on the sink, tears flowing freely. She'd never cried this hard in her entire life. *Please let it end soon,* she thought again, glancing at her haggard face in the mirror.

But as she prepared to examine her tear-stained face, she jumped back, stunned that the mirror had apparently lost its reflective quality. Instead, she saw Candace as if the mirror in the guest room had been switched. She touched the glass, shouting, but her daughter remained on the bed, pressed against the headboard, her arms tied to the posts as she sobbed and screamed. Seeing her baby in anguish almost killed Marian on the spot.

"Candace," she wailed, stroking the glass, imagining herself touching Candace's face.

But then a figure appeared near Candace. It was armed with a knife. Marian blinked, looking again at what appeared to be red hair cascading down the figure's back. What had happened to Rachel's black hair? She was startled, horrified as the redheaded figure moved forward, slicing at Candace's cheek with the knife. Her cuts were slow and deep, and Candace squealed in pain as the blood ran down. Marian pounded on the mirror, yelling, doing everything she could to call attention to herself. She needed this to stop.

As if on cue, the knife halted at the sound of Marian's voice. The redheaded figure turned toward the mirror. Slowly, her neck creaked in place, Candace quieting as the knife retreated.

Marian screamed louder as the figure came closer so she could see its face, the melted skin hanging in clumps as its yellow teeth snarled. Where lips should be, there were none, adding a chilling effect. What was this? Just when things couldn't get any worse, now there was another entity? Marian shook her head backing up from the sink, from the mirror, quaking wildly. But before she could hit the cool, tiled wall behind her, she felt claws on her back.

"Don't worry, your daughter's in good hands now," the voice whispered on Marian's neck, and she didn't have to turn to know Rachel was behind her. She could hear it in her dripping, raspy voice.

"Kill me already. Stop this," she uttered, turning to face the girl. It would be better to die than to see Candace in pain. "Let the others live."

Rachel's face lit up. "Why would I do something silly like that? Debts must be paid, after all. Debts the family owes. You know something about that, don't you?"

Rachel tapped her long, pointy fingernails on the tile wall behind her, clacking them lightly, one by one. She breathed in Marian's face, and the smell was of decaying, burning flesh. Marian bit her lip to stop from crying. She forced herself to stand strong and tall even though she wanted nothing more than to crumple to the tile floor.

"Yes, Marian. I know. I know all your dirty secrets in this family. All of them. We're not so different, you and me. Are we? We both have quite the evil side. We both don't know when to stop. We take it too far."

Marian shook her head. "You don't know anything." Her breathing intensified as she stared at the being before her, her eyes glued to the decaying pox on her face.

"Oh, but I do," she replied, and from her pocket she pulled out an ice blue lighter that made Marian gasp, took her back. Rachel flicked it, over and over, until the flame was eye level between them.

"Just a flick of the wrist and all your problems were gone. Or so you thought. No one would ever know."

"I was protecting my daughter," Marian said, shaking her head. "He was a monster. I had to protect her."

"Protecting her from what? What kind of mother puts her daughter through that? She could have died," Rachel replied, her voice growing in intensity. The flame kept flickering, and Rachel pressed it against Marian's cheek, singeing it. She cried in pain, not just from the flame, but from the memories.

She'd done the right thing. He was abusive. He was dangerous. He wouldn't have stopped. She needed the police to believe that he was dangerous. When he'd shown up that night, he had planned to take Candace. A flick of the wrist, a drop of the lighter, and it all changed.

No one needed to know it was her flick of the wrist, though. It worked perfectly. They thought it was him. Candace thought it was him. The police thought it was him. He was forced to disappear, alone, to leave them alone.

"You could have killed her!" Rachel shouted, and Marian jumped. She took a step back, leaning against the smooth top of the sink. "You're all the same. A mother's love—what a fucking joke. You all deserve to die."

Rachel's hands were around Marian's throat now, the lighter gone. She closed her eyes, hoping it was the end. *I'm sorry, Candace,* she thought, realizing she'd die with that secret on her heart. *I did it all for you.*

As she waited for the choking death to come, though, it didn't. Instead, there was a burning pain on her wrist, on her arm, on her neck. She squealed, opening her eyes to realize Rachel had the rusty scissors again, and they were slicing into her flesh. She kicked and screamed. She pleaded with Rachel to kill her. The final stab of the scissors didn't come, though.

"I'll be back," Rachel said when she'd made the final, superficial cut. Marian could hardly care. The blood was oozing down now from both arms. She was in so much pain, she wanted to die.

Rachel left, and Marian sobbed on the floor. She could let herself die, let the blood loss kill her. But then she remembered Candace. She pulled herself up on the sink, anguish and burning pain racking her body. She glanced in the mirror to see if the portal to Candace's room was still visible. And that's when she saw the single vision that gave her hope.

Candace was alone. And Marian's precious fighter of a girl wasn't giving up. Because somehow, the girl had managed to free one of her hands from the restraints.

Maybe they would survive this thing after all, she told herself, crawling toward the shower to tend to her wounds and get ready for the next round.

Chapter Twenty-Four
Anne
1955

Time fades all feelings to a certain extent, and for Anne, the guilt over her lies was assuaged as summer turned to fall. With Rachel tucked away in the haven of Redwood, the family went on. Anne didn't talk about that fateful day with her mother, convincing herself that life without Rachel was better for everyone. That Rachel was getting the help she needed.

That she'd done what needed to be done. They all had.

Her father had visited Rachel once, but Anne and her mother stayed away. It was easier to forget about the twin sister who had haunted her life, who had created so much havoc. It was also easier to avoid looking into the eyes of the sister she'd betrayed.

Was it treachery, though? Maybe Rachel didn't really try to kill their mother this time, but wouldn't she have tried in the long run?

Anne busied herself with school, with dates, with cooking. The family had a peaceful Thanksgiving, unmarred by Rachel's antics. The town stopped talking about her, as if she were dead.

In many ways, being committed to Redwood Asylum was like a slate wiped clean for the rest of the family. The forgotten building buried in the forest was like a black hole—those who went there became enigmas to be forgotten and ignored by the rest of the town. Rachel would spend her days there, tucked away where she couldn't damage anyone.

As the snow collected on the ground in December and the holidays marched toward them, Anne smiled at the thought of new family traditions. Peaceful nights drinking hot chocolate. Tree trimming. Cookie baking. With each day that passed, Anne got closer to the life she realized she should have had, if only Rachel hadn't been born.

And then the phone call came, the final blow. The final tie.

The breakdown of her father. Even her mother shed a copious amount of tears, although it was difficult to tell if they were genuine. Her mother, after all, had become a great actress over the months, painting on the pitiful face in public if someone should mention Rachel.

When they pulled Anne to the living room and sat her down to tell her the news, though, Anne felt nothing. Numbness. Blankness. She nodded, listening to Dad say phrases like "suicide" and "inexplicably found with scissors" and "emotional pain." She processed what he was saying, that Rachel was permanently gone. The wretched girl had taken matters into her own hands and ended it on a cold, winter night in her room at Redwood.

But as her mother continued to sob, Anne stared blankly ahead. She felt nothing. How had she felt nothing at all? Shouldn't she have sensed something? True, they were clearly never close, but Anne hadn't felt a blip on her radar, a tingling, anything. Even now, the knowledge that her twin was gone forever—it didn't even startle her. Her stomach didn't drop. Tears didn't well. Apathetic was the only word for it.

Alone in their room that night, she wondered if maybe she was the monster after all. With a shudder, she finally drifted to sleep, swearing she heard Rachel's voice whispering in the darkness. Her dreams were not peaceful that night, filled with images of scissors, red, and a rusty ornament she had never seen before.

Chapter Twenty-Five
Anne

Tears fell down her wrinkled, craggy face as she sat on the bed, staring out the window. Her daughter's screams and Candace's sobbing echoed through the house, but Anne knew she was powerless. Just like Rachel all those years ago.

She thought about how not long after the news of Rachel's suicide came, her mother had come into the room and handed her that package, wrapped in paper. The Christmas bell that she'd dreamt of the night Rachel killed herself came to fruition, and with it came a glaring realization that Rachel would never leave her, not completely. That there would be no peace. Most of all, Anne came to believe that maybe peace wasn't what she deserved.

After the first contact with the Christmas bell, when that twine burned through her finger and she felt that odd sensation, she knew there was something stronger than real life at play. And that night, she'd opened her eyes in the darkness to see a specter in her room covered in splashes of blood, her familiar black braids and soulless eyes leaving little doubt of who it was. Rachel had worn a smile that was too wide, that suggested to Anne that all was not well. That all would never be well again. She'd wrapped the ornament and put it in a box, shoved it in the back of her closet to be forgotten.

And it was forgotten—just like Rachel. The photographs were removed from the walls. The memories and nightmares of her subsided. Anne went on with her life. She got married, had Marian, and lived a normal life. She forgot about Rachel for the most part, thought that it was all settled. Still, every year when Christmas came, she would remember the whispers, the bell, and the twin sister she betrayed. She would drown the thoughts out with an over abundance of beautiful ornaments and Christmas carols and presents. She tried to cover up the past with shiny gold bows and glittering signs of the season.

It worked. As time passed, she was lulled into the belief that Rachel was gone, that her own soul was unmarked, and that all was peaceful and bright.

When she'd married Charlie, she'd carefully stowed the boxed-up ornament away, a relic she wanted desperately to be rid of. Still, it was the last piece of her sister, and Anne feared to destroy it would be to obliterate any piece of goodness, of forgiveness Anne might have. She knew that when she died, she'd have to answer for her sins. She hoped someday she could find a way to make it right.

For decades, she'd thought it was over. But now, Rachel had returned to exact her revenge, and Anne was horrified of what that would really mean—not for herself, but for her daughter, for Candace. They were the only ones who mattered now. They were the innocents in this fiendish game of chess that Anne knew she was about to lose.

The snow fell outside, and Anne was temporarily soothed into a harmonious psyche as she inhaled, slowing her heartrate. She'd made so many mistakes in her life, but so had Rachel. She'd been given a wicked sister. What was she supposed to do with that? Who could really blame Anne for how it turned out?

The room remained silent, but the hairs on the back of Anne's neck stood up as goosebumps marked every inch of her flesh. She gulped in air, the stagnant and decaying quality assaulting her nose.

She was here. Anne didn't need to turn around. Perhaps the twin sense had come in after all, just a little late. Footsteps inched toward her. The floor creaked. A giggle sounded. Anne stood, turning to face the truth, the doom, the reckoning. Rachel stood confidently; the deadened smile was familiar but also distant.

"Miss me, Sister?" the raspy voice croaked, and a tear slid down Anne's cheek.

"Stop this madness, Rachel. Stop it now. Why, after all these years?"

The being didn't speak, didn't sputter. The smile she'd worn for days now faded to a thin line. Anne saw the remnants of the saddened sister she'd once known. Rachel stepped forward, but Anne didn't quake with fear. The longer Rachel was here with her, the longer Candace and Marian were safe. That was all that mattered now.

"Madness? You want to talk about madness? What about the madness of locking me away in that hellhole all those years ago? What about the lies you told? Do you have any idea how much I suffered from your lies, Sister?" Rage smoldered in the questions. Anne noticed that Rachel clenched her long, slender fingers into fists.

"I'm sorry," Anne muttered, the words genuine. She *had* been young and foolish. Rachel was wicked, but Anne hated that she'd had to play the role she did.

"Sorry? *Sorry?* That's what you have to offer? Do you know how much I suffered? The treatments that were simply torture in medicine's disguise? Do you know how they abused me, how many times they raped me? Do you know what's it like to live without an ounce of hope, without any vision for any type of future that isn't cold?" Her questions were frenetic now, her mouth frothing. She stepped closer to Anne, who stepped back against the frost covered window.

"All those years, Sister, I was abused by the family. But it was nothing compared to the life I lived in those walls at Redwood. I wouldn't wish it on my own worst enemy. And what were you doing? Thinking of the sister you condemned on a lie? No. You lived your life. Had a child. Had grandchildren. That should have been my life."

"This isn't making it better, Rachel. Hurting others doesn't make it better."

Anne's words were soft and empathetic, but they had the opposite of their intended effect. A roar burst from Rachel's throat.

"I'm not here to make it better. I'm here to make you pay. All of you deserve to pay." Her bloodied teeth dripped with spit. Slobber cascaded from her mouth as she creeped closer, her hands clutching Anne's neck. Her decaying face smelled of burning garbage and mold, her breath suffocating Anne. But it was the look in her eyes that chilled Anne, that incited a deeper fear. Rachel's eyes were empty and soulless, but in the back of them, it was as if there was a fire burning. Anne was certain she could see the flame.

Rachel leaned down and bit into Anne's cheek. The old woman screamed in agony, a pain she'd never known. She could feel her flesh tearing, the searing pain and squirting blood stirring nausea and sobs. She implored Rachel to stop, the teeth sinking in and devouring her face.

"Kill me. End this," she begged.

Rachel spit a chunk of her cheek on the floor beside her, and Anne closed her eyes.

"It's funny, Sister. Because that's what I wanted more than anything, too. Unlike you, I was brave enough to carry it through. You aren't, though, are you? What are you afraid of, after all? There's power in death. Your daughter and granddaughter will find that out soon."

"Please, God, no." Anne sobbed, sinking to the floor as Rachel let go. Laughter burst from Rachel. Blood gushed, sticky and hot, from her cheek.

"God doesn't hear you. He quit listening to a sinner like you long, long ago, you stupid bitch."

"Why now? Why after all this time?" Anne asked, needing to know the answer to the question that had plagued her. She felt woozy but willed herself to stay upright and conscious. She needed answers.

The grin on the disturbed face widened. Rachel shrugged, giggled, and walked away, perhaps knowing her failure to answer was more torment than the truth.

Vomit rose in Anne's throat. Rachel really was out for vengeance. She was Rachel's plaything now. They all were.

Anne's fingers went to her cheek, feeling the sticky, oozing blood. Her whole body shook, and she wanted to pull herself up to assess the damage in the mirror. She was too afraid. Rachel was right. She was weak. She wasn't brave or strong. But she needed to be. She needed to stop this witch, somehow, some way.

She pulled herself up in agony and pain, her head unsteady and her mind whirling. But now that Rachel had left, Anne knew she would be tormenting Marian. She could hear her daughter's screams echoing through the house, the shouts resonating in Anne's head like off-tune, eerie tintinnabulations.

Anne's life was slipping away, but she needed to be strong. She needed to find a way to sacrifice herself in order to save her daughter, her granddaughter. She would face the reckoning for her sins later, but they didn't deserve to die.

Chapter Twenty-Six
Marian

She was losing too much blood, and Marian hated to think about how quickly infection would set in. Her arms were covered in gaping wounds. She needed to clean them and wrap them if she was going to survive. She could hear her mother's screams now and could see Candace fumbling with the last of the restraints through the mirror. Her daughter kicked her way free. With any luck, her daughter would escape. With any luck, Marian would find a way out, too. Her hands trembled from the sight of all the blood, but Marian assured herself it was nothing a little soap and water couldn't fix. She bit her lip at the prospect of the water seeping into the slices, knowing the pain would be unbearable. But she was strong. She was the fixer, after all. Skinned knees, splinters, bug bites. She had always repaired it all. Now, she would just have to fix herself.

Even if she did survive, what would she tell the hospital? That the same being that murdered Rosalie and Eva was now going to kill them? She'd heard the stories of what happened to the town's crazies—Redwood Psychiatric Hospital, a thinly veiled cover for an asylum of terrors, was the town's guarded secret. After all, Rachel had been there and look at what happened to her. There was no way Marian was ending up there, not now. Not ever.

"Think, Marian," she ordered herself as she started the shower. They'd tried to figure out how to appease Rachel. Now, that hope was gone, obliterated with the swish of the scissors. She had to figure out how to stop her. After all, it was Christmas Eve. If they could just survive tonight and tomorrow, maybe the ghost of the horrifying past would settle, would return to wherever she'd been. Maybe they'd be okay after all.

Life had dealt Marian so many rough hands, but she'd always won in the end. Even after Joe's stunts, she'd managed to keep them safe. She thought about the drinking, the abuse—she'd protected Candace from that. She'd protected her from a father who was one step shy of psychotic, willing to hurt his ex-wife and only child in an inferno of rage. And when her plan to get him locked up backfired, she'd kept careful watch over her shoulder all these years when the bastard disappeared into thin air. Perhaps he knew that the psychological warfare of never knowing if he would show up again would be worse. Still, she'd survived it all. She would survive this, too. They all would.

Pain blinded her. Her skull exploded as the water hit the gashes. It felt like the water was hitting down to the bone. She steadied herself on the slippery tile wall, willing herself not to pass out.

"What do you want from us?" she asked senselessly, cleaning the wound with the hot water, rubbing soap delicately on it and trying to distract herself. The gash on her left arm was the deepest, probably worthy of stitches.

"What do you want?" she repeated into the steamy air. It felt absurd, bartering with a non-existent entity. Still, the gashes on her arms, the death of Rosalie and Eva made it evident. Just because the rest of the world wouldn't believe her, it didn't make it any less real.

There was no answer. Marian shoved back tears as she let the hot water stream over her face. What would become of them? What terrors awaited them? The worst part was there was nowhere to go, nowhere to hide. They'd awakened the past. Now, they couldn't shove it back down until Rachel got what she wanted.

And what would that be? What revenge would satisfy a depraved girl who had suffered so much? It was crazy to think about her mother doing that to her own twin sister. Still, Marian wasn't there. She knew what it was like to live with a monster, yet to have no one believe in the validity of the statement. You never knew someone's pain, someone's struggle until you actually lived their life. That was something she'd learned the hard way.

She massaged her neck, exhaling, wishing for once someone else would solve the problem. Someone else would step up. She let the suds cascade down around her, inhaling the steamy water. The steam filled her lungs, and she felt cleansed, hopeful even. A hot shower always was her escape.

She listened to the pinging of droplets against the shower door, and for a moment, she thought she could hear the familiar carol. "Silent Night" faintly echoed through the room—or maybe she was truly earning a place at Redwood.

No, if she listened and concentrated, she could hear the melancholic Christmas tune. Were there carolers outside? She hoped. It would do Anne and Candace good to have a slice of peace, of happiness, even in the midst of the pain and fear. They'd need their mental strength if they were going to survive the night. She leaned her head back, listening to the notes, lulled into a state of false peace. But then, even with the water hot and her skin scorching from the droplets, a shiver ran through her.

She suddenly knew she wasn't alone. Terror overtook her, usurping her momentarily peaceful escape. It suddenly seemed senseless to be in the shower in the middle of it all. She should have used the time to make a plan, to figure it out. It was too late now.

She turned to look out into the ceramic terrain of the bathroom, but her eyes stopped short. They fell on the foggy shower door, where a black shadow blocked out the light. A scream built in her throat, but she told herself to stay calm.

She closed her eyes and opened them again, hoping against hope the vision would go away, that her tired mind was just extra weary. But when she opened them, the shadow had been replaced by the pale face blackened by scars and shadows. Rachel's face pressed against the shower glass, blood streaking from her eyes onto the door.

"It's your turn," the whisper barked at her before thudding her head on the glass. Marian scampered to the back of the shower, her arm still aching from the last cut from the scissors. She was a strong woman. She'd had to be. Still, the thought of the inevitable pain, the feeling of those rusty scissors in her skin had her shaking like a weakened, pitiful creature.

Before Marian could scream, before she could shout her last, Rachel had whipped open the shower door, flinging it back like it was a piece of paper. She cornered Marian, the hot water still beating down.

"Please, please don't hurt them," Marian said, knowing her life was finished. The only thing she worried about now was the safety of Candace, of Anne.

She should have told them to leave. She should have sent them far away. She should have done a lot of things, she realized as Rachel's sharp teeth peeked out from her sickening, red grin, blood dripping down her face.

Rachel smirked, pausing right in front of Marian's face. "Don't worry. It only hurts for a while," she said. And then, she was upon her, the rusty scissors dragging a line straight over her neck. The steaming water mixed with the hot, piercing sting of the scissors as Marian stared into the ghoul's face, the notes of "Silent Night" fading into an off-key version as it all went white.

Chapter Twenty-Seven
Candace

C andace's fingers were shaking so badly, it was difficult to finish the job. She tried to tell herself to stay calm, to breathe. She told herself she could save them if she just focused. Hearing her grandmother's and mother's shrieks and cries, though, wasn't helping her nerves. The situation was dire. She needed to get out. But how? And where had the redheaded monster gone?

Her fingers finally untied the fabric from her left wrist as tears fell. She wiped her eyes, which were blurred, and took a deep breath through her mouth. Armed with her baseball bat, she debated whether she should try to escape through the door in order to get to her family quicker or risk the drop out the window and a broken leg. She stood for a perplexing moment, eyeing the two options. She dashed to the window, the bat making contact with the glass. It didn't shatter. She hit it again, harder this time. Still no crack.

"Please," she shouted to the silent air. "Please." Again and again, the bat pummeled into the window, but it was as if it were covered in a magic film. Frustration and rage built in her, overpowering the fear momentarily. And then the giggle from the hallway dropped a cloud of despair on her. She froze, turning to the door.

The white door creaked open slowly, and her heart lodged itself in her ragged throat. She backed away, her shoulders hitting the wallpapered corner as she shivered.

Footsteps. They were leaving her room now. The door hung wide open, inviting her into the darkened hallway. It seemed odd to question whether she should go now. This was what she wanted, yet something sinister taunted her. It couldn't be over this easily. She could see a flickering of lights, perhaps from the hallway or the kitchen. Taking a deep breath, she fought all screaming urges to stay put and trudged forward, bat in her hand. She edged her feet forward, tiptoeing down the hallway in a scurrying fashion. She was desperate to end this thing. She willed her breathing to slow down so she could hear better, but her senses were already heightened from adrenaline. Water beat down from somewhere in the house. The shower? Was the shower running?

Abandoning all pretense of caution, Candace dashed down the door, tears stopped as her new mission was ahead of her. She needed to save her mother. But as she approached the bathroom, another noise distracted her: the cries of her grandmother.

Two doors. Two choices again. Candace's mind raced with what to do. She had no idea. But hearing the shower, she assumed maybe her mother was okay. She dashed to Grandma Anne's door, Candace's old bedroom. Holding her breath, she wriggled the knob.

It opened, to her surprise and terror.

"Grandma?" Candace asked, and at the sight of her grandmother on the floor, her face a mangled, bloody mess, Candace screamed.

"Go. Go get your mother," Anne choked and sputtered, crawling toward the open door. Candace helped pull her grandma to her shaky feet as fast as she could. Blood flowed from a wound on her grandma's face, but Candace didn't have time to obey her shaking hands and queasy stomach. She followed her grandmother's shouting pleas and dashed back to the bathroom door.

"Mom?" she bellowed, trying the knob to the bathroom. It didn't work. She pounded on the door like she had so many times growing up, bothering her mother for something silly like a question about cookies or asking for the car keys. How many times had her mother sacrificed her own wellbeing, her own happiness, for her? And how many times had Candace taken it for granted, all that woman had done to protect her?

"Mom?" she yelled again, louder this time. The shower kept running, water pounding against the tiled wall or tub like a downpour. There was no answer.

She twisted the doorknob again, harder this time. It rattled underneath her death grip but didn't budge. Locked. Panic set in and warped her already crazed mind. She pulled and yanked, violently shaking the door and shouting for her mother. She kicked the door now, her foot aching as her foot made contact with the strong wood. Anger surged through every kick, through every contact with the white wooden door. Her toe hurt, probably broken, but it didn't matter. None of it mattered.

Just as she was sinking to the floor, about to give up, the bloodied Grandma Anne crept closer. As if at Grandma Anne's command, the door gave way. It creaked open so painfully slowly that there was a pause, an anxious silence in the hallway as the two women drank in a mutual breath. They needed to see inside the bathroom but at the same time they couldn't bear it. They knew what they would see before they even opened the door.

The steamy air billowed out of the space in a rush for freedom. When the hot fog lifted, Candace's body shook as she noted all of the flecks of blood. Her eyes focused on a dazzling pattern on the ceramic tile nearest her. Maybe it had just been flecks from a simple wound, she told herself. All was fine. All was okay.

Growing up, Candace had believed nothing bad could happen on Christmas Eve. It was the one night of the year she felt safe. Santa came on Christmas Eve. There was a man in the house, a good man, who would keep them safe from her father's violent nature. But now, as she crawled to the tub, still yelling for her mother, she knew that just like Santa Claus, her belief in the safety of Christmas was forever slaughtered.

As the curtain peeled back and she saw her mother's body, stabbed and mutilated, a rusty pair of scissors planted deep within her chest and her throat slit, Candace fell. Her cheek smashed against the cool tile as she soaked herself in water, blood, and the tears of a life forever changed yet again.

"One too many," a voice croaked, but this time, as she scrambled from the floor, she realized it was Grandma Anne who was in the doorway, chanting the words with tears and disbelief in her eyes.

"One too many, indeed," another voice echoed from beyond, and Candace knew the fight wasn't over.

Chapter Twenty-Eight
Anne

She didn't have time to grieve for her daughter, for the pain. Anne turned to face the assailant, the fiend who had destroyed Anne's entire world again and again and again. She stood, that disgusting smile, the blackened scars on her face. Still, in the white, she was what some might call impossibly beautiful.

Anne did not see radiance or beauty, though. She saw a beast as she always had.

"I told you you'd pay," Rachel cawed into the air. Anne could hear Candace's sobs behind her. She stood between them, no longer afraid but needing it to be over.

"You stupid girl," Anne said, stepping toward the being. Candace begged her to stop, but Anne saw clearly what needed to be done. She walked forward. "One too many. Always one too many. Even now. No one loves you, mourns you. No matter what you do, you'll always be the one no one cares about." Anne stared straight ahead, seeing the anger bubble in Rachel's deadened eyes. Her grin faded slightly as she squeezed the scissors tighter.

"You're the one no one loves, Anne. Look at you, miserable and weak. You're the pathetic one. At least I was someone to talk about, to remember. You think Mother loved you? She liked that she could control you."

"Weak girl, wicked girl. No one loved you," Anne repeated, the anger palpable in the air.

"You'll fucking pay," Rachel roared, and Anne stood still, closing her eyes and waiting for the end to come. It didn't. Anne stood untouched, but sensed a scuffle behind her. Candace wailed. Anne turned around to see her worst fear.

Rachel had Candace around the throat, the scissors pinned to the soft white flesh of Anne's granddaughter's skin. Rachel had taken them all, had taken everything from her. And now she was going to take Candace, too, and leave Anne vilely, unabashedly alone.

"Such a pretty girl. Shame to see her defiled, isn't it?" Rachel laughed, scratching the rusty scissors into Candace's cheek, leaving an X of blood as the girl writhed in agony. "They're all going to be gone, Anne. And then who will love you? You'll be all alone, just like you deserve." Rachel spewed the words through gritted teeth, giggling in a muffled way as she sliced and diced at Candace, blood spewing.

Anne scrambled forward, but Rachel kept backing up. Back farther and farther, into Anne's room, dragging Candace as she cut and sliced, the girl bleeding profusely. Anne's stomach fell. It was too late.

Rachel taunted and laughed, her giggles mixing with Candace's screams in a soul-torturing way. Anne begged, shrieked, moved her aching bones toward the scene. She had no idea what to do, how to stop it, but she knew she needed to save

Candace. She was weary and weak, her frailness apparent. She hadn't saved Rachel. But her granddaughter was an innocent. She had to try.

As she moved forward, Rachel now holding Candace hostage against the window in the room, ready to take her into the next life, Anne crossed the room to her dresser and pulled open the top drawer. In a moment of lucidity and strength, she remembered them.

The scissors. These were gleaming silver, brand-new and ready. A few days ago—had it really been only a few days? —she'd used them to wrap the gifts tucked away for Candace. Now, they would be used to give her an even greater gift, although it would be one paid for with blood.

"It's over, Rachel," Anne announced, turning to her sister. She opened the pair of scissors, Rachel still slicing at Candace. Her granddaughter's eyes were squeezed shut in pain as she moaned, her breathing shallow. There wasn't any more time.

Anne didn't pause to think about the pain. She sliced her wrist expertly, deeply, as if she had always been meant to do it. The metal bit into her veins and blood gushed. Over and over she sliced, the burning hot mixing with the faintness she felt as she was slipping away.

"It's over," she whispered, staring as Rachel dropped the rusty scissors, as Candace fell to the ground, a crumpled wreck.

She lay dying, waiting for what would come. She hoped to see Charlie or Marian, comforting faces to tell her that her pain was over and that she'd finally done the right thing. That she'd finally ended this nightmare.

She saw neither. As she slipped away into the great unknown, her only company was the decaying girl with a wide grin whistling "Silent Night" off-key. And Anne knew that there would be no peace. There never was for the wicked.

Chapter Twenty-Nine
One year later

She hugged the pillow to her chest, looking out the frosty window as the snow fell. Terror threatened to usurp her, but she quieted it. She needed to be alert, awake. She didn't want them dulling her senses with drugs again.

It was Christmas Eve. She might come tonight, Candace realized as tears welled. She rocked herself back and forth, back and forth, the nervous energy within her desperate to escape. She'd seen the redheaded figure here a few times, in her room. She never spoke, just pointed at Candace, at the vent, and was gone. Candace shuddered, confused by her presence, wondering who the girl was. But she'd learned not to ask too many questions. Curiosity really did kill the cat—and her grandmother, mother, and everything she believed about life.

They'd tried to hide it from her, the date. The staff, the nurses, especially the new ones, all thought she was too fragile to know what day it was. They worried she might relapse. Who could blame her if she did? They hadn't seen what she'd seen. They hadn't experienced the terror of being prey to something no one even believed.

And there was the problem. No one believed her. She'd landed here, thanks to an anonymous donor who took pity on her and paid her way, because she simply couldn't get anyone to believe her. The cops were out looking for a serial killer. Too bad the serial killer wasn't someone they could arrest.

Over and over, she'd told her story. What choice did she have? They were all dead now. Eva, Rosalie, her grandma, her mother. She had no one left, no one to trust. She had no one who would be able to help her. She was left to solve it on her own—because they all just thought she'd gone batshit crazy.

Maybe she had, in truth. Some nights, when Candace sat awake listening to the moans of the other residents at Redwood, she wondered if she had, in fact, made it all up. Because after that night when she'd crawled for her life down the dirt path, bleeding and terrified, she'd never seen her again. Rachel had vanished, just like her grandmother, just like her mother. They were gone, as if they'd never existed. At least she had pictures to prove her mother and grandmother had been there. But what was there of Rachel, other than the demonic ornament? She wondered what happened to it. To all of it, actually. Not that it even mattered. She'd signed it all over to her grandmother's church in her hometown. She hadn't wanted any part of it. If and when she left this place, she would never go back to Maple Street. She would go somewhere far away where Christmas didn't exist because Christmas had stolen everything from her.

She looked away from the window, bile rising in her throat. She hated windows, mirrors, glass of any kind now. She was always terrified that she would come back. That was the worst part, the part she was all too familiar with. Wondering when the reign of terror would begin again.

She'd gotten a postcard from him, after all these years. He'd heard about everything, which meant he'd been keeping tabs on them. How many times when she'd been growing up and heard a noise outside had she been right? How many times when she felt like she was being watched was he lurking about? How many times did they falsely think they were safe when they were nothing of the sort?

He had disappeared into the night that July day when he'd tried to kill them, her mother and her. He'd flicked the match and disappeared, never to be seen from again—or so they hoped. They had survived, thanks to her mother. Her mother had always been the strong one, the survivor. At least that was the narrative that Marian had told. Now, Candace knew, the survivors, the ones left, got to tell the story. And the story wasn't always the whole truth.

The postcard had come a few weeks ago from an unidentified address. It seemed benign enough, which was why the staff shared it with her delightfully, probably hoping it would cheer her. On the front was a sandy beach, shimmering sand that looked beautiful and hot to the touch.

On the back, a simple note:

I'm not the monster, Candace. I didn't set that fire. You know that in your heart.

I love you. I want to help you.

Dad

What did he mean, he wasn't the monster? True, in the past year, she'd learned that monsters were real and were much darker than any human, even her father. Still, she looked at the words, feeling all alone. Was it true? Was there more to her dad than she knew?

Her mother had said he was abusive. That he had tried to kill them. She'd seen the fire. She'd been there, been pulled from the burning building. But the police had never found the culprit. They'd tried to pursue her father, but he'd disappeared. Vanished into the cold night along with her faith in him.

Her mind raced, hugging the pillow tighter. She'd had nothing but time to mull it over since she'd ended up at Redwood. *It can't be. He's a monster. Mom wouldn't lie...*

But then she thought of her grandmother and all the secrets the sweet, elderly lady harbored. All the secrets that led to their destruction. Could it be possible? Could her mother have hidden the truth? And did it even matter?

She rocked herself on the bed, clinking her head against the wall, wondering if anything actually mattered at all.

We live in these perfectly constructed worlds where every choice we makes leads us down a path. Or so we think. Because one day, a monster, a being, our own dark past comes for us and shreds everything we thought we knew.

Candace closed her eyes, wondering how it all ended for her. Wondering if it could all end. Understanding how Rachel must have felt for the first time.

Alone. All fucking alone.

Tears dripped down her hollow cheeks. She heard nothing but her own breathing, but the soft pelting of ice chips on the window, and in the distance, soft music playing.

Silent Night. Holy Night. All is Calm.

For a moment, she was terrified to open her eyes. She keep them shut, her breathing intensifying. But when she finally found the courage to open them, the room was empty. All really was calm. But nothing was bright. Nothing could ever be bright again, could it?

She sank her head down onto the stiff cot, alone in the world, drifting to a sleep that she wished could be the long sleep because, as she'd come to learn, there really was nothing in this world or the next worth fighting for. And that was the saddest fact of all. That was enough to make any girl, black-haired or otherwise, go mad with a hunger for revenge.

A soft grin painted itself on her face as she thought about the possibilities before drifting off to a sleep that wasn't filled with nightmares or dreams or anything in between.

Epilogue

He saw her stamp out the cigarette on the sidewalk right outside the door before scolding the two wild beings on either side of her. They lowered their heads as the woman pointed at them in turn. He could read her lips, the stern warning not to touch anything.

He'd been in this job long enough, though, to know that if you bring a kid to a pawn shop—or even an adult for that matter—they're going to touch everything. His signs could be damned. Of course, the "You break it, you buy it," sign sometimes came in handy.

It was an odd place to bring two children, two girls, who couldn't be more than five. But Cody Connor never questioned things anymore. He'd lived a long life. He'd seen it all. The pawn shop, if not super profitable, at least provided entertainment in his old age now that he couldn't carry on with his younger life's transgressions.

The mother waddled in, shoving her sunglasses on top of her vibrant orange-tinged hair that either needed washed or less hairspray. The two ducklings followed in a row behind her, their matching black bowl cuts and mischievous grins telling him they must be twins. She had her hands full.

"Hi, welcome to Cody's Pawn Shop. What can I do for you?" he asked with a smile as the girls scattered, their eyes alight with all of the junk. One man's junk, though—

"I need to get some cash for this," she said without an air of dignity. He liked them straightforward, though. No one came to a pawn shop with much dignity.

"Looking for cash for the holidays? Santa need a little help?" he said softly. Usually women like her weren't his typical clients, but with the holidays right around the corner, he'd seen an uptick in mothers desperate to play the holly jolly role.

"Something like that," she said. "How much?"

Her eyes scattered, looking for her two children. At the moment, their hands were at their sides. They were touching only with their eyes for now. He was impressed by their restraint.

He haggled with her over the Jade gemstone ring. Not really significant to pull in a lot of cash. Still, he knew he could turn a quick profit on it. Some foolish guy in a hurry would buy it with the right sales tactic. He could convince them it was all the rage.

They went back and forth, the woman stanchly debating its worth, that she wouldn't be taken for a fool. The girls had a strong mother, at least. He hoped they would appreciate that fact. They settled on the price, and he was getting the payout when one of the bowl-cut heathens wearing the sugary smile of a girl walked over, clutching something.

"Mama, look! An ornament for the tree. Look how pretty."

The mother looked down. "Looks kind of creepy to me."

He turned from the counter to see the girl holding a bell-shaped ornament. It was rusty and in serious need of some paint. There were scratch marks and some weird saying carved into it along with a creepy silhouette of a girl. It had seen some years, for sure.

He shuddered, looking at the child holding it up. She didn't seem bothered by it, though, smiling as she held it. Her sister grabbed it from her, also smiling as she touched it.

Weird.

When his assistant, Mark, had gone to that garage sale up north, he'd come back with boxes of junk from some old house. Some tragedy had struck the family and the property had been left to a church. They had a huge sale with the contents of the house. Mark had come back with all sorts of dinnerware and sofas, and boxes of holiday décor. Cody had almost thrown some of it out, pissed that his assistant clearly hadn't been a very good student. But something about the rusty bell had called to him, had made him want to pick it up.

He shuddered, thinking back to how he'd been alone in the storeroom when he'd touched it. Thinking of the jolt that went through him, the images, the feverish chill. He'd thrown it down, then laughed at himself. Apparently, he'd had too many of those pills he'd gotten from Mark. He was losing it.

Looking at it, though, in the little girl's hands, a foreboding gloom overtook him again. Suddenly, he didn't care if Mark thought it looked vintage or that he could sell to a collector.

"Take it," he said. "Merry Christmas."

"Really?" the little girls asked, jumping up and down with the childish naivete that led them to believe they'd really won a treasure.

"Positive," he said, finishing up the sale and handing over the payment.

The mother thanked him, and he nodded, feeling guilty though. As they left the store, one of the black-haired twins dangling the ornament, a chill ran through him, a distinct shiver. He watched them fade out of sight, the family in search of cash and an easier lot of it. The little girls with the rusty Christmas bell.

He tried to shake it off, but as the bell on the door tinkled once more, he swore he heard something in its notes. A humanistic voice, a shrill whisper.

"One too many."

The words reverberated deep within. He shook them off, storing the Jade ring in the jewelry case before turning back to the cash register to finish the day's work. He counted the drawer, focused on the task. He'd forgotten about the girls, about the bell, absorbed by real life and his present circumstances to the point that he didn't even notice the black-haired girl in a nightgown drifting past the front window.

Nor did he see the second figure, this girl with blonde hair, trailing far behind, a saddened look in her eyes as the black tears dripped down her cheek, as she followed along solemnly to a new existence.

Acknowledgements

To my husband, for always supporting my dreams and making me laugh. I love you so much.

To my parents, who taught me that books and writing are important, I love you. Thank you for always helping me find confidence in myself, loving me, and pushing me to chase my passions.

Thank you to the many readers who have taken a chance on a small-town author. I appreciate every single one of you for investing in the stories of my characters.

And to my best friend, Henry, thanks for always being there on the long days of writing and editing to make me smile.

Did you love *The Christmas Bell: A Horror Novel*? Then you should read *A Tortured Soul*[1] by L.A. Detwiler!

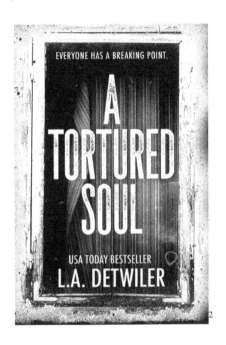

From USA TODAY Bestseller L.A. Detwiler comes a sinister horror with jaw-dropping twists.Everyone has a breaking point.At twenty, an unplanned pregnancy seals Crystal Holt into a marriage to the abusive Richard Connor. After a stillborn birth, Crystal insists they have the baby baptized postmortem. A cynic, a drunk, and a poor man, Richard has other plans. When her monstrous husband tosses the baby into the woods to be forgotten, Crystal instantly spirals. After beating her within an inch of her life, Richard does something

1. https://books2read.com/u/b55v5A

2. https://books2read.com/u/b55v5A

else he's done before—he disappears. This time, however, things feel very different...With her husband gone, Crystal battles with the demons of abuse, dark childhood memories, and a declining mental state worsened by horrific nightmare sequences. As the story unfolds, it becomes clear that something's not quite right about the way Richard disappeared this time, and Crystal is in more danger than ever. After all, not all of the dark secrets belong to Richard.Will Crystal be able to escape from a lifetime of torture unscathed, or will she succumb to the dark secrets she's fallen prey to before?A twisted page-turner that will disturb even the toughest horror and dark thriller fans...

Read more at www.ladetwiler.com.

Also by L.A. Detwiler

The Diary of a Serial Killer's Daughter
A Tortured Soul
The Christmas Bell: A Horror Novel
The Christmas Bell: Rachel's Story

Watch for more at www.ladetwiler.com.

About the Author

L.A. Detwiler is USA TODAY Bestselling author and high school English teacher. Her debut thriller, The Widow Next Door, is a USA Today and International Bestseller with HarperCollins UK/Avon Books. Her second thriller, The One Who Got Away, released in 2020 with HarperCollins UK/ One More Chapter. The Diary of a Serial Killer's Daughter released in 2020.

L.A. lives in Pennsylvania with her husband, Chad, their five cats, and their mastiff named Henry. Her writing has appeared in several women's publications and online magazines. She also writes romance under Lindsay Detwiler, including her popular Lines in the Sand Series.

Join her Readers' Club with this link: http://eepurl.com/gkZ2Sf

Read more at www.ladetwiler.com.

CPSIA information can be obtained
at www.ICGtesting.com
Printed in the USA
FSHW010502010921
84451FS